Pirates of New York

Pirates of New York

Gene Anderson

First Printing, 2026
Amorphous Publishing Guild
Buffalo, NY USA
www.Amorphous.Press

Contents

If there's one thing I want the reader to know, it's that this is simply a *fun book*. It is not trying to be historical fiction or take itself too seriously. It's an entertaining story, and despite some amount of suspension of belief, you can easily picture it all in your mind, feel the excitement, and maybe laugh a little. Even the cover art is meant to convey the feeling of the narrative rather than to represent scenes from the book.

I enjoyed editing it, even though it had to be cleaned up after being converted to text from scans of paper that came out of a typewriter many years ago. Two of the books I published for Gene Anderson were biographical in nature, but this is the second work handed to me from his old keepsakes. Gene wrote this work as part of an informal writer's club while interned at the California Correctional Institution (CCI). His other clubmates were entertainer Rick James, a bank robber known as "Red Joe", and a gangster nicknamed "Keith Caper". This could be a story in itself. This is also when he wrote the trilogy of "The Adventures of Captain Star and the Amazing Dr. Zuntor", and other works that may yet be published.

Having the scans of the original draft of this story, dated May 1996, I want to note that an inscription gifts it "To Dad / Love, your Son / Gene Poo Poo Man Anderson / 1997 / Happy Father's Day".

It was a long way coming, but Gene and I are pleased to put this out for the world to see. He hopes it inspires his friends who have always wanted to write, who may not have believed in themselves until seeing what can be achieved by someone they know. I am glad to have been one of the people to help make this possible.

Ken JP Stuczynski
Editor / Publisher, Amorphous Publishing Guild

Chapter 1

It was a hot sweaty night in the Caribbean, off the coast of Bermuda — right at the Bermuda Triangle, circa 1743. A small pirate ship with a flag bearing crossbones and skulls was blowing in the direction of a secret inlet, where many of the outcasts and rejects from all over the world had gathered for their safety.

In his Captain's quarters, we find a raunchy old man with a big pot belly and long, grey beard. Heavily armed, he always carried five flintlock pistols in his waistband, and sported a long, golden-handled sword and a golden-handled dagger. He was leaning over a big table, looking into a box full of jewels and coins. He was also studying a map of the island area.

We find him rubbing a long scar on his face, as he exhaled a big smoke ring from his long, golden pipe. He was one of the most ruthless pirates alive. Born with the name Edward McHopkens, the only son of a noble Scots family. He had turned bad at an early age. He stole a ship and was able to keep a crew to man his ship by breaking into jails and hand-picking men. In time, he had become one of the most feared pirates on the high seas.

He, himself, alone, had killed over one hundred and twenty-seven men. Seventy-nine he personally hanged. He had shed so much blood on the high seas that he was given the name "Captain Red Dog" — a name that he personally loved.

On another ship, only a few miles off the coast of the secret island of the pirate haven, we find the humble captain, Sir Richard Ball. As his ship cruised through the still waters of the islands, he was in search of outlaw pirates. He was on a mission for the Queen of England to stop all the unwanted pirating in that area.

Walking on the deck of his ship with a telescope to his eye, looking across the horizon, Captain Ball said to his first mate: "Mr. Peters, I have a strong feeling that before morning, we're going to have some luck."

"Yes, Captain, I also feel something strange about this night. Did you see the moon, Captain? It's fuller than I've ever seen it before! Maybe it's a sign that we're going to catch up with that blout, Captain Red Dog, and put him in irons ! If we're really lucky, we might even catch that renegade, Captain John Flenn", said Mr. Peters.

Captain Ball replied, "Let's not get our hopes up too high, Mr. Peters. We both know that John Flenn is an unpredictable fellow. Just when we think we got him, he just disappears."

"I know, Captain ... But sooner or later, his luck is going to run out."

In his mind, Captain Ball was thinking about how Captain John Flenn got on the wrong side of the law. As a young man, John Flenn was a cabin boy to Captain Ball. He was never without questions about the high seas. Captain Ball knew that John Flenn was born to be a great seafaring man. He took much time out to educate John about the sea. He taught him all he knew about being a great sea captain. In time, he worked his way up to the first mate position. How proud Captain Ball was of him, until one night back home in England, while on shore leave, John Flenn was in a small inn, celebrating being home from a long voyage. A group of off-duty policemen came into the inn. John Flenn and his men were sitting around a table singing songs and drinking. Surrounded by all the women and girls who worked in the inn, there gas one young girl who was very beautiful. She was sitting on John Flenn's lap, kissing him. "Oh John", she said, "You're the best seaman in all England."

With a smile, John answered, "Only in England, my dear? Why not the whole world?" Then everybody began to laugh. They all were having a great time, singing and drinking.

One of the policemen was in love with the young girl sitting on John's lap. His face turned red with envy. Jumping up and turning over his table, he said "I've had enough of this crap! He rushed over to John's table and grabbed hold of the girl's arm; he pulled her off his lap, pushed John, then threw her on the floor. Still holding her by the arm, and twisting it, said, "Listen mate, this is my woman, and I don't appreciate you fooling around with her! If you swabs know what's good for you, you'll get out of here while you're still in one piece!"

Before he could get it out of his mouth, John was onto his feet, and with a fast right hand, John knocked him to the floor. As the policeman lay there unconscious, John picked the young lady up in his arms and said, "Let's go up to my room before things get out of hand.

As he walked up the stairs carrying her, out of the side of his eye, John could see the other policemen picking up their friend. Pouring rum over his head, his friend said, "Are you alright Sir?"

Still dazed, the policeman saw John carrying the young girl in his arms. He yelled, "I'll get you for this!" Then, not thinking John could see him, he pulled out his pistol, but to his amazement, John turned, and with one fast motion, shot the policeman dead center between the eyes.

That started the entire inn (John's men against the off-duty policemen) to fighting and shouting at one another. The fight became more and more violent until all seven of the policemen and two of John's men were dead. The inn was a wreck — tables were turned over, women were screaming and crying, and blood was everywhere. A night that started out to be so much fun ended up with so many men killed or wounded, and, by the looks of things, John Flenn was going to get all the blame.

"Let's get out of here," John said to his men who had not been killed in the fight. So they began to run through the back door. More police rushed into the inn. Seeing what had taken place – blood everywhere and all the dead bodies, some of which were policeman – they began to open fire on John and his men as they were trying to escape. With a lucky shot, one of the pursuing policemen shot John in the back. Collapsing to the floor, John began to crawl to the back door. Samooya, John's right-hand man, looked back to see where John was. Not seeing him, Samooya ran back to find John on the floor bleeding and unconscious. Grabbing him and throwing him over his shoulder, as if he were light as a feather, Samooya quickly ran away, ducking gunfire from the police.

All night, the police searched for John and Samooya. The streets were alive with police and their dogs. They were looking everywhere for the two renegades, kicking down doors, waking people up out of their beds, asking everyone if they had seen these two men. The next morning, there were posters all over town offering a $10,000 pund reward for the capture of John Flenn, "dead or alive".

In the meantime, Samooya, running with John on his back, knew it was only a matter of time before John would die. He had to get help! He could hear the dogs behind him, as he made his way through the woods. Closer and closer they came, until he was cornered. There he was, standing at the edge of a cliff, looking down at a fast-moving river. He was panic-stricken, not knowing what he should do. The doge and the police were gaining on them! One of the policemen shouted with a loud voice, "There they are!" Seeing the two fugitives, they began to fire their guns at them.

Samooya, with John on his back, knew they didn't stand a chance. So, without hesitating, he jumped off the high cliff into the raging river below. As the pursuing men looked down from the cliff into the river, one man said to another, "Well, I guess that's the last we will see of those two. No one could live through that." They turned and walked away.

Completely out of breath yet holding onto John, Samooya swam to the other side of the bank. As soon as he reached the other side and managed to crawl up out of the water, he passed out. Samooya and John both lay there, unconscious.

Walking with a basket in her hand and picking wild flowers was a small, young lady with the smile of an angel. Her name was Jessica, and she lived close to the river in a little farmhouse with her elderly father. As she slowly strolled down by the river, to her surprise, she saw the two men laying on the bank. Filled with apprehension, she walked over to them. She leaned over to see if they were alive. That was the very first time she saw John Flenn: her heart was about to jump out of her chest, then, unexpectedly, she felt something grab her by the ankle. She screamed and tried to pull away, but couldn't.

It, was Samooya. Falling to the ground and kicking, Jessica screamed, "Let me go, let me go!" only to be grabbed around the mouth by Samooya.

"Don't be afraid, I won't hurt you, " said Samooya. Taking his hand from over her mouth, he said, "This is my friend; he's been hurt. We need help. Looking at Samooya, Jessica, scared out of her wits, was wondering where did this big black giant of a man come from. There he was — a huge, black man from off the Gold Coast of Africa, standing seven-foot-three, weighing about three hundred and fifty pounds, with a bald head and wearing a large golden earring. All muscle, no fat, straight monster. But there was a look in his eyes as gentle as a puppy's.

Swallowing her fear, she asked, "What about your friend? He looks as if he needs help."

"Yes, I've got to find some place to patch him up", said Samooya. Without considering the danger she might be putting herself in, she said, with no hesitation, "I don't live far from here. You can bring him to my house; he'll be safe there."

Back in England, at the Hall of Governors to the Queen, Sir Richard Ball is sitting by the Queen, becoming despondent as he listens to the charges against John Flenn. Shaking his head, he sadly spoke, "Your Majesty, how can this be, that a lad as fine as John Flenn would do all that killing without reason? You know, there have been people who've said he was only defending himself, Your Majesty."

Sitting across the table from Sir Richard was the Chief of Police, Sir Guy Hunt. He and Sir Richard had never been friends, because Sir Guy knew that the Queen always gave Sir Richard too much power. But this time, Sir Richard, by letting his young first mate (who was always getting into trouble) run wild, had gone too far. 'Your Majesty, don't let this oily-tongued Sir Richard talk you out of justice! This man killed seven of my best men. And, if you're going to have law and order, this man must be hanged!"

As the two men argued, the Queen shouted, "Stop! Both of you, STOP! Sir Richard, I know that young man John Flenn. I've seen him grow from a young boy into one of the finest men in the Queen's Navy. I know that you, yourself, taught him all that he knows, Sir Richard. And, he's like a son to you. But, he still has to pay for what he's done. It's like Sir Guy says, if we let him get away with this, all of England would have no respect for the law. So, as much as it hurts, I'll have to put the stamp of 'Outlaw' on him. That will be all there is to it." Then she got up, called her Royal maids, and walked toward her chambers.

Turning, and looking at Sir Richard, Sir Guy quietly said, "This time you'll have to do as I say. And, I'm ordering you to bring him in. No matter what it takes, or how long it takes. Dead or alive, it makes no difference to me. Just bring him in! Either it's his head, or yours!"

Back in the farm house, laying on a bed, was John Flenn. Standing at a fireplace with a red-hot poker in his hand, Samooya was looking over at Jessica. She was trying to help his friend with a pan of hot water and a rag in her hand. She was wiping the sweat from John's head. Walking over to the bed and looking down at his friend, Samooya said, pulling the bandage off the wound, "We're lucky the ball went right through and out the other side. All I have to do is stop the bleeding with this hot poker."

Jessica asked, "Have you ever done this before?"

Samooya, with concern written all over his face, replied, "Yes, but never one so bad. If he moves, and this poker touches the wrong place, he'll die."

Although he was in a deep sleep, John wakes up and says, "Where am I?" He tries to get up.

Samooya says, with tears in his eyes, "I don't want to do this, little guy, but I don't have much choice."

With that, Samooya taps John lightly on the chin, and out he went. Then, with the skill of a doctor, Samooya pressed the red-hot poker into the hole in John's body. He holds it for a few seconds, then throws it back into the fireplace. He grabbed some clean rags, bandaged the wound, and then tied him up. Turning to Jessica, he said, "Now all we can do is wait and pray."

All over England, reward posters were up: "WANTED, DEAD OR ALIVE, JOHN FLENN AND SAMOOYA." The entire populace was dreaming of collecting the reward.

After about a month, John was up walking about and wondering what to do next. Knowing sooner or later they would have to move on because people had been seen roaming around near the farmhouse.

"John, where are you?" called Jessica. "I've been looking all over for you. What are you doing out of bed?"

As she ran up to him, her heart and eyes were filled with love. "Yes, my sweet," said John, thinking about how precious she had become to him in such a short time. "I was just taking a short walk, and thinking. I'll have to clear my name. We'll have to be leaving because it's too risky for you and your father for us to be here."

Jessica, still gazing into his eyes, said, "I wish you would never leave. I've been so alone until you came into my life. No, I simply cannot bear the thought of losing you.

"No, no, my darling, you'll never lose me, " he said as he held her in his arms.

Looking into her eyes, he slowly kissed her for a very long time. They continued to hold each other tightly as the sun began to slowly go down behind the horizon.

Then, from out of nowhere, the sound of gunfire rings through the air. "What's that?" screamed Jessica. "It sounds like trouble back at the house!"

"Where's Samooya?" asked John.

Jessica, frightened, started to run through the fields. "He's down by the stables with the horses. That means my father is home alone! Let's get back to the house. He must need help!"

When arriving at the farmhouse, they see men on horseback, setting fire and destroying everything in sight. One of the terrorists was dragging her father behind his horse by a rope. He also was the one giving orders to the others, shouting, "Don't leave anything standing! Burn this place down to the ground! We must find those two dogs!"

Running from the pasture where the horses were, Samooya got there just in time to tackle the man who was dragging Jessica's father. In a rage, this giant of a man knocked him and the horse both to the ground. Then, he picked the man up over his head and threw him into another gang of men, knocking them to the ground also.

John, grabbing his sword, like a wild man, began to take men on, two at a time, leaving a trail of dead or wounded men as he made his way to Jessica's father. The battle appeared to slow down as the two men began to even the odds. Samooya, with the strength of ten men, grabbed a fence pole from out of the ground and began to swing it at the men on horseback. He was knocking the men out, and knocking the horses down.

Jessica ran through the confrontation and helped John drag her father under a wagon, out of the way of the battle. John, like a streak of lightning, dropped men with his sword until there were only a few left to fight. Samooya ran over to some of the survivors, (there were five of them in a group) and wrapped his huge, long arms around them. He squeezed them until he broke all five of their backs at the same time. When the other men saw this, one said to the others, "Let's get out of here, we need more help!" The terrorists, afraid for their lives, rode off down the trail as fast as they could.

Running over to Jessica, both of them knew as they looked down at the old man that it was hopeless. He was taking his last breath, saying, "I'm trusting you, John, to take care of Jessica. She will need both of you now." Then he turned his head and closed his eyes.

"No, Papa, don't leave me! No Papa, NO! " she cried.

John put his arms around her and picked her up. He said, sadly, "Don't cry, my sweet, I'll be here for you always, and forever."

The three of them, after burying her father, got onto three of the best horses and rode towards the beach. Being careful not to be seen, they made their way down to the docks. John said to Samooya, "I've got to get on board our ship and talk to the men about getting out of here and back onto the high seas."

"But how are we gonna do that?" asked Samooya, "with all those guards posted in front of the ramp of our ship?"

Snapping his fingers, John said, "I've got an idea... do you remember when we were in China? There were some acrobats. One of them picked the other one up by the foot, then threw him on top of a platform. Do you remember, Samooya?"

"Oh, yeah, I've got it! I think I can throw you all the way onto the top of the main deck if we can get the attention of the police away from the ship."

Let me take care of that, said Jessica. "I'll get their attention, and when you're on board, I can double back to this side, and you can throw me a rope and pull me up."

"Maybe it'll work," said John. "We don't have any other choice... Okay, what do you have in mind, Sweetie?"

" Just watch this." She rearranged her hair, pushed up her breasts, and calmly walked right in front of the policeman. As she passed them, she gave them a sexy look that made one guard say to the other, "Let's give it a try." They both turned and walked behind her.

As the police walked out of the area, they were not able to see the two men when they made their move. John said to Samooya, "Here' s our chance." Then John put his foot into Samooya's hand, and in one great motion like a sling-shot, John was thrust through the air like a rocket, landing on top of the main deck.

Samooya saw that his friend was safely on board, and he realized he also had a chance. He saw a chain hanging from the ship down to the anchor, saying to himself, "Come on, Samooya, you can do it." Knowing it was about twenty-five feet away from the dock, Samooya, holding his breath, got a good running start and took off like a bird. It was a jump that would have been impossible for an average man. But Samooya was much more than any average man. Grabbing the chain with his fingertips, Samooya pulled himself up to the top of the deck and climbed over the guardrail. Then, as he crawled across the deck, he met John who was also crawling to meet him.

John smiled, saying, "Samooya, you are fantastic! Now, I'll take this rope and climb on top of that main sail. You hold this end of it."

A minute later, Jessica had slipped away from the two policemen. The men were still out of sight and looking for her. Back on the dock, by the ship, looking up, hoping to see a signal, she saw John on top of the mainsail with a rope in his hand. As she stood there, with her mouth open, John swings down in a big loop, and scoops her up in his arms. Before she could blink her eyes, they were both back on top of another sail.

"How did you do that?" said Jessica. Giving her a big smile, then a kiss, John said, "Experience, sweet lady. Experience!" They began to descend to the deck. As Jessica looked down to see why they were moving so smoothly, she saw Samooya slowly releasing the rope through his hands.

Now they were all on board the ship together. Trying not to be seen by the police, the three of them crawled across the deck. They slipped down into the hole where John's crew was being held. And they began to creep down the old wooden steps. There they were — John's crew, locked up like rats in a trap.

The first man to see them was John's old Chinese cook. "Me'sa John ... Mes'a John, over here!" said the cook.

"Whose got the keys?" John asked his cook.

"They made a guard room out of the map room, Mes'a John. And the keys are in there on the wall. Be careful! Really bad men, Mes'a John, Bad men!"

Slowly, the three of them crept down the dimly lit ship until they were at the guard room. Cracking the door and peeping through it, John could see a table full of policeman, drinking and smoking. John said to Samooya, "Are you ready?" He shook his head yes, and in a flash, the door was kicked open. Caught by surprise, the policemen were soon under control.

Throwing the keys to Jessica, John and Samooya put the subdued guards in irons. Unlocking the door, Jessica led the men up the steps to the main deck. John and Samooya rushed topside to join their men. The crew stayed down, crawling, so as not to be seen by the remaining police. They started picking up clubs and anything they could get their hands on. After a signal from John, the crew began to take over from the guards. John and his crew were running and scrimmaging; they were fighting for their lives. It was a treacherous and wild battle. Jessica, too, was in the middle of all the fighting, causing as much damage to the police as anyone.

Not long after the fight was over, the anchors were pulled up from the water. The sails were unrolled. There was a strong wind in the sails, which was moving their ship safely out to sea.

"Where must we set course for, John? Or should I say, 'Captain John Flenn?'" said Samooya, giving John a big smile, as he turned the wheel.

Still holding onto Jessica, John said, wearing a proud smile, "Due West, Mr. Samooya! Due West!"

After a time at sea, the little ship was pulling into a small island in the Bermudas. That's where Captain John Flenn became the boss of a small island, soon to be the stronghold and secret hideout for all the bad men of the sea. And all under Captain John Flenn's control.

As time went on, he became a legend on the high seas. One day, at an inn owned by Jessica and John Flenn, Captain Red Dog and his men were back from a raid on some merchant ship that netted them lots of booty. The crew was drunk and breaking up things, as well as fighting each other. Captain Red Dog was in a back room talking business with John about paying taxes for hiding out on his secret island.

"I'm not gonna pay you nothin', John Flenn!" Red Dog looked John in the eye and said, "It's about time that someone else takes over this island."

"Well, if you don't want to pay, you and your men will end up in a hole in the ground," said John.

"Are you threatening me, John Flenn?"

"No," answered John. "I'm promising you. Now, give me my share! And, you can get off my Island."

With fire in his eyes, Red Dog pulled out one of his pistols, only to have it taken away from him and hit on top of his head with it by John Flenn.

"Samooya, take this sea dog, along with the rest of his useless crew, and throw them off our island!"

"Right, Boss," said Samooya.

Not long after a bloody good fight with Red Dog's men, they were rounded up and put onto their ship and made to sail out of the harbor, into the vast sea. From that day on, Red Dog lived for a chance to take the island and kill Captain John Flenn. Each time they saw one another's ships, it was always war!

Chapter 11

As Captain Sir Richard Ball walked to his state room, he was shaking his head in sorrow, saying to himself, "What a waste. Lousing up a good man like John Flenn." There was no choice; he had to do his job. After all, he was the Senior Captain of the Queen's Navy.

As they were sailing around some island down by Dead Man's Reef, the sound of cannon fire filled the air. Running through the door was Mr. Peters. "Captain Ball! I think we've got both of them!"

Running out of the door and onto the deck, looking through his telescope, Captain Ball saw two ships firing at each other. "Yes! You're right, Mr. Peters! Yes! It looks as if we might get both of them this time! Hoist full sails for more speed, Mr. Peters."

While keeping up a barrage of cannon fire at the other ship, Red Dog was yelling to his men, "We've got them on the run, lads! Keep firing! Don't stop!"

John Flenn and his men were on the run. "Head into that fog bank, Samooya! Maybe we'll be able to get behind them and take them by surprise!"

"Aye, aye! Captain!"

John starts giving sailing orders, and Samooya repeats the orders, as the crew hurriedly responds.

"Left full rudder... Steady as she goes... Good Samooya! Now all we have to do is wait. We'll just let Red Dog pass us by, then we'll be able to get behind him."

"Great move, Captain," said Sanooya, "We'll get rid of that cur once and for all."

As the three ships slowly sail through the thick fog, Samooya said to John, "I can't see a thing, John. How about you?"

"I know... But neither can they. All we have to do is wait, so we can get a good shot at them."

Captain John Flenn and his crew slowly floated in the calm sea, in the midst of a thick fog. Although they were unaware, they were in the center of the Bermuda Triangle. Suddenly, as if a big wind was blowing the little ship in a huge storm — it began to go round and round. The powerful circles of water got smaller and smaller, tighter and tighter, and faster and faster! They were in the middle of a giant whirlpool! Helplessly, the little ship began to sink to the bottom of the sea! The men were clinging to each other, and to anything else they could grab hold of! Round and round the little pirate ship went, until it hit the floor of the ocean!

Then, just as it began, it stopped. The little ship was pushed back up to the top of the sea. How strange! No one was drowned or hurt!

"What happened, Captain John?" asked a frightened Samooya.

"I don't know, but let's get out of this hellish fog so we can see! Right full rudder, Mr. Samooya, then hold her steady."

"Aye! Aye! Captain!"

Slowly, the little ship appeared from out of the dense fog into the bright sunlight of a clear and beautiful day.

The men were trembling and looking at one another saying, "Don't you feel strange?"

One man turned to another, and looking dazed, he asked, "Mate, do you feel well do you feel as if your body has changed?"

"I don't know what I feel, but something is wrong! I just know it!" answered his friend.

Samooya, also confused, asked, "What course shall we take, Captain?"

John, searching through his telescope, could see nothing except calm water and clear sky. "Due West, Mr. Samooya, it looks like we must have lost them in the fog."

"Captain Ball, what happened to John Flenn's ship, Sir? It seems it just disappeared."

Captain Ball, looking a bit confused himself, answered. "I don't know, Mr. Peters. That fog lifted, and I can see clear to the horizon, and there's no ship out here but us. It's very strange Mr. Peters, very strange indeed!"

"But we had both of those ships in our gun sights. Red Dog's ship got away on the edge of the fog. Remember Captain? We saw him running away. But John Flenn slipped into that fog bank and never came out again!"

One of the other sailors interjected, 'It's as if his ship ran off a big riff, Captain, and went under."

Captain Richard Ball answered, "I don't know, but we'd best try to find Red Dog's ship. Maybe we can get him!"

Meanwhile, aboard Red Dog's vessel, he was speaking to his first mate. "Well, it looks like Captain Ball must have gotten that rascal John Flenn for us, Matey. Today must be our lucky day — now the seas belong to us, all by ourselves," laughed Red Dog.

Walking around the deck thinking and looking through his telescope, Red Dog ordered, "Set a course for John Flenn's secret island! Since he's gone down to Davey Jones's Locker, I can take over, and show those lazy weaklings who's really boss! Come on, men, let's go have some fun!" He laughed like a demon, and with the anticipation of riches, his crew got busy.

Chapter III

At NASA, men were monitoring a new satellite that had been placed in orbit by Space Shuttle Endeavor.
"It looks like our new reconnaissance satellite is doing its job better than we expected, Sir," one of the men said to his boss.

"Yes, Paul, I think we have something to celebrate. But first, let's see what kind of pictures we can pick up from around the Bermuda area."

As the technicians made their adjustments, Paul turns from looking into his monitor and says to his boss, "What great pictures, Sir. We can zoom in on a car and read its license number all the way from space. This new satellite is going to be great for our country's defense."

As the group of men gathers around the monitor screen, celebrating, one man, looking at the screen, points his finger and shouts out, "What's that?" Everyone turned to look.

"I don't believe it! It ... it ... it ...looks like an old pirate ship!"

Paul stammers in amazement, "No! It can't be! Maybe it's a prop ship from some movie or TV show."

Another man says, "Whatever it is, TV show or movie, it's in trouble!"

Paul, getting himself together, says, "Ah, come on now, let's not forget that the Battleship Missouri is having war exercises in that area today."

On the bridge of the battleship Missouri, the Captain says to his chief officer, "Are you ready to try out our new short-range guns, Lieutenant Gaither?"

"Yes Sir, Captain."

"Ready on port side," said the Captain.

"Ready on Fort Bide, Sir," answered the gunner over the intercom.

"Fire a test round from cannon one," said the Captain.

"Cannon one Fire, Sir." And with a loud bang, the Missouri began to fire.

Zooming over the top of the sails of the little pirate ship, the shell crashes into the water with a big explosion, making the water splash into the little ship; rocking it from side to side as if it were in a hurricane. All of this was quite unexpected. Holding onto the wheel of the ship, Samooya said, "Captain, what's going on? Someone is shooting at us, and I don't see them!"

"I know! And, if we can't see them, we can't fight them!" answered John Flenn.

Then another explosion hit in front of the little ship, rocking it, and almost turning it over. Water was splashing everywhere into the little ship. "Captain, it must be the devil from the deep!"

The men were crying out, "Save us, Captain! ... What* s going on, Captain?"

Samooya yelled, "What'll we do? Captain?"

John yelled back: I don't know what's going on, but full rudder, sixty degrees!"

"Aye, Aye, Sir!" yelled Samooya. Then, turning the wheel with a sail full of wind, the little ship slowly sailed out of range of the big guns of the Battleship Missouri.

Back at NASA, with the use of the new satellite, the entire scene was being monitored by a room full of people.

"I can't believe my eyes, Sir," said one of the men to his boss.

"Neither can I, but we'd better do something quick! Get in touch with the White House! Hurry! Get them on the phone."

Men were shouting orders all over NASA's control room. Phones were ringing and everyone was in a panic! One of the men said anxiously, "Someone better stop our battleship from firing before we kill some of those movie people!"

"Those movie people don't ever think they have to check with anyone before they do their thing, " said another man.

Within seconds, the White House was on the phone. One man ran to his boss, handing him a cellular phone. "The White House, Sir."

"McNeil, Sir. It looks like we've got a problem, Sir."

A voice on the phone said, "What kind of problem?"

"Some movie people have gotten into the range of our testing some new weapons on the Battleship Missouri, off the coast of the Bermuda Islands, Sir... Yes, Sir! ... They're in the Bermuda Triangle, Sir!" After listening, he said, "Yes, Sir — We need to stop our ship from firing, and pick them up! We're going to have to move them out of the area as soon as possible!"

The voice over the phone answered in an angry tone. "Not only that," said the voice, "tell the Captain of the Missouri to impound that ship and put those people under arrest!"

Answering the voice, McNeil said, "Yes, Sir! Got it. Over and out!" McNeil hung up and turned to the monitor. Shaking his head, he said, " Somebody put me in touch with the Battleship Missouri. I need to talk to its Captain."

Not long afterwards, a voice came over the loudspeaker saying, "The Captain of the Missouri is on the phone, Sir."

"Hello, Captain, this is NASA. We have orders from the White House for you to stop firing at once!"

"Why?" asked the Captain of the U.S.S. Missouri. "We've been preparing for these tests for months, and we have just gotten started."

"I know," said the voice over the phone, "but it's a matter of life and death. It seems that some Hollywood movie people have gotten into your firing range and are about to be blown out of the water! So, your new orders from the White House are to cease firing! Then pick them up on your radar screen, track them down, pick them up, and tow that little imitation of a pirate ship into port! Also, put those Hollywood hotshots under arrest!"

"Got you, NASA! Over and out!" said the Captain. "Right full rudder," he ordered. The big battleship began to cut through the water on its way to pick up the little pirate ship and its crew to place them under arrest.

"It's a good thing you have fast thinking, Captain. I thought we was goners for sure," said one of the pirates.

"Well, it's gonna be a smooth ride back to our island, since We've given the slip to both Red Dog and Captain Richard Ball," said John Flenn.

"Yeah, John," said Samooya, "I'm still thinking about that Devil from the deep. I wonder what happened to Red Dog and Captain Ball? Maybe that devil of the deep got the both of them and their ships!"

As soon as those words came from Samooya's mouth, the Battleship Missouri sailed across the horizon, into the sight of everyone on the little pirate ship. John Flenn, never in his life having seen anything remotely the size or shape of a battleship, was shaking in his boots. He said to his men, "We've only got one chance — man your guns and fire at will!" The little ship began firing, but the battleship was well out of range.

Back on board the Missouri, the Captain was looking at the whole scene on a monitor that was hooked up with the new NASA Satellite. Seeing the little pirate ship on the screen, it looked as if it were a TV show. The ship looked like a toy firing at them, compared to the giant-sized battleship. Smiling, the Captain said, "Those Hollywood folks went all the way toward making that ship look authentic."

"Fire! Put more powder in! And more fire to the guns!" ordered John Flenn.

The Chief Gunner replied, "I don't know if they can take any more, Captain. They're red-hot already."

"Well, just keep firing!" yelled John Flenn.

As the big battleship came closer, the cannonballs began to drop very close to the big ship. "Sir! They're firing real rounds at us! What should we do?" asked one of the men.

"Maybe we should fire a small round across their bow," said the Captain. Moments later, a big boom came from the battleship's guns, which went across the bow of the little ship. This caused the little ship to rock and almost capsize.

"That devil ship is about to blow us out of the water, Captain! What now?" asked Samooya.

"We'll have to run up the white flag, but when they try to come aboard, we put up a fight like they've never seen before!" said John Flenn.

"We're pulling alongside their ship, Captain, and the men are ready to board her, Sir," said the Lieutenant.

"Very Good," said the Captain. "Pass out some automatic weapons to your men. If you get any trouble out of them, just fire over their heads, then move in on them."

"Yes, Sir!"

They prepared to board the little ship, which looked like a piss-ant next to an elephant.

All the men on the little pirate ship stood there with their mouths open. Looking up at the giant battleship, not believing their eyes. The crew was all frightened and began to comment, "Wow! What is it, Captain?"

"It can't be real..." They were all speaking at once.

"I don't know," said John, "but whatever it is, ITS BIG! ! !"

The men on the battleship were looking down over the side of their ship, not believing their eyes. "What in the hell is this little ship doing out in this deep water?" queried one of the sailors.

"Man, it looks like something from out of one of those movies about pirates," said another.

Finally, the Lieutenant and a small crew were in a speed boat headed swiftly across the water toward the "MOVIE BOAT."

"Captain! There's a strange-looking thing coming this way, moving fast!" Samooya was obviously agitated. "I've never seen anything move so fast, Captain! Look! Look! What the blimey damn hell is it?" he shouted. The pirate crew were momentarily all scared speechless!

"Steady men," said John Flenn. "It won't be long now. The crew on the pirate ship stood there with swords and pistols in their hands, ready to jump the strange men in the speed boat as soon as they came on board their ship!

Soon, the little speedboat pulled alongside the pirate ship. Even though small, it was almost as large as the little pirate ship itself. With a loudspeaker booming from the speed boat, the Lieutenant said, "This is the U.S. Navy! We are asking to speak with the Captain of this ship."

John stepped forward and spoke, "That would be me, Captain John Flenn, at your service, Sir!"

The loudspeakers' booming voice sounded again, "Tell your men to drop their weapons and come on board our vessel! This ship is being confiscated by the United States Navy!"

At the sound of the loudspeaker booming and hearing the voice of the Lieutenant, the crew of the pirate Ship began to tremble. "What kind of sea monster is this?' "I've never heard any kind of sea creature speak before!"

"Captain John! Tell us what to do, Captain John." Normally, these brave sea-going men could not be frightened by anything or anyone. But now, all they could do was turn to their beloved Captain John Flenn. However, by this time, Captain John himself was at loss for words; he didn't know what to say or do!

The speedboat pulled closer to the side of the little ship. The Naval crew was armed with automatic weapons, while the pirate crew was armed with swords and musket rifles. All the men, from both ships, were utterly confused.

One of the seamen on the speedboat said to the man standing next to him, "Man, I must be dreaming. This can't be! At first, I thought this was some Hollywood thing, but this ship and these guys look like the real thing!"

The only thing one of the sailors could manage to say was "Wow!" Another sailor said, "This can't be any kind of Hollywood or movie thing — there are no cameras, or lights, or any other kind of movie equipment on board!"

"Wow ! Wow! Wow! " the other sailor continued to mutter.

"Alright, men," said the Lieutenant, "Let's round them up!" At once, like a well-oiled machine, the men brought out folding ladders and began to climb the side of the ship, all boarding the little pirate ship all at the same time. John Flenn had never seen a maneuver like this in all his years at sea. Before anybody could make a move, the U.S. Navy had landed on the deck of the pirate ship and had the drop on everyone.

Not knowing what those strange-looking weapons were in their hands, Captain John Flenn, knowing nothing else to do, ordered his men to attack. With a loud scream from the pirates, they began to charge with their swords waving in the air. Seeing this, the Lieutenant gave the order to open fire. He yelled, "Fire over their heads, men." Like lightning, the automatic guns began to spit round after round over the heads of the pirates. Not able to understand any of this, John Flenn, Samooya, and all of the pirate crew fell to the deck, covering their heads and closing their eyes. "Okay, men, that's enough! Cease firing!"

After the smoke cleared and the men from the speedboat stopped firing, they began to laugh at the funny sight of the pirates lying on the deck, with their heads covered up, and their eyes closed. The Lieutenant and his men began to round up Captain John Flenn, Samooya, and all the others. They put them on board the speedboat, and were off to rejoin the Missouri, with the little pirate ship tied behind it and being towed to the battleship.

Once on board the big battleship, the men from the pirate ship were looking around at everything. Their eyes were opened like a kid in a candy store. Both crews were looking and touching each other. Neither of them could believe what they saw!

"Captain, this is the Captain of the ship we commandeered at your orders, Sir," said the Lieutenant.

The Captain replied, "Very good, Lieutenant Gaither; you're dismissed."

"Thanks, Captain, but, if it's not too much to ask, Sir," pleaded Lt. Gaither, could I have a chance to talk to him along with you? Please, Sir."

Looking at his 'First Mate' with a smile, Captain Nash said, "I don't blame you, son. If I were you, I wouldn't want to leave the room either. Permission granted."

As the Captain was about to introduce himself to John Flenn, the phone rang. The sound of the phone made John fall to the floor. Laughing to himself, the Captain picked up the phone and said, "Hello, Captain Nash speaking... Oh, yes, Sir. He's right here. As you say, Sir." He hung up the phone and turned to look at John. Next, he looked at his Lieutenant and said, "You won't believe this, but that was the President of the United States. "

"What?"

"Yes, you heard me right, and he wants me to appoint a man to accompany them to Washington, D.C. ... to the White House. How would you like to be that man, Lieutenant?"

"Hell yes, Captain! - I mean, uh, uh, Yes, Sir!" corrected the exuberant Lt. Gaither.

"Now, you, Sir..." Turning his attention to John Flenn, he walked over to his special place under his bed where he pulled out a bottle of red wine. He poured the three of them a glass, and said to John, "What is your name, Sir?"

Captain John, pulling himself up tall, said, "I'm Captain John Flenn, once with the Queen's Royal Navy, Sir!"

"Huh?! Captain Flenn? Did I understand you to say Captain John Flenn? *The* famous pirate of the Bermuda Islands?" the incredulous Captain Nash asked.

"The one and only, in the flesh," said John.

"Hold it! Don't tell me you are him!" commanded Captain Nash. He and his ship went down to the bottom of the sea, in a whirlpool, in the Bermuda Triangle, and were never seen again! I think that was around 1743 ... That couldn't possibly be you."

Captain, said John, "All I can say is the truth about who I am... Answer me this, if you can: how is it you know so much about me?"

"Well," Captain Nash answered, "every boy that ever wanted to go to sea heard about the great Captain John Flenn."

"I don't understand," said John, and as his inner turmoil became more complex, he asked, "What year is this?"

"It's 1998, replied Captain Nash."

"1998?" Captain John was so confused with the strange sights and happenings of the past few hours, he thought he must be losing his mind!

Captain Nash was very much confused himself, but he replied to Captain John's query about the year, "Yes, so you simply can't be the pirate Captain John Flenn!"

Lt. Gaither interrupted: "Excuse me, Sir, if you don't mind my saying this, Sir, did you see, on the monitors, what happened when we picked them up?"

"Yes," said Captain Nash, "not only me, the whole world saw it! It's been on all the news; It was even on CNN all day. That's why the President said to bring him to the White House."

Captain Nash, shaking his head and looking at John Flenn, said to him, "Well, even if you are not that famous pirate, the entire world thinks you are. So, if you say you are Captain John Flenn, then you are Captain John Flenn! Anyway," concluded Captain Nash, "the Smithsonian Institute, and the media, will be meeting us as soon as we reach port."

Back in Washington, D.C., at the White House, the President and his cabinet were at a table discussing the most astounding historical discovery of all time. They were planning on how to get votes in the coming election by using the pirates to their advantage. "Mr. President," said one of his cabinet members, "as soon as the people from the Smithsonian verify that these are true pirates, and through some freak of nature, survived all these years, we're in the driver's seat!"

Chapter IV

"Hey, Dad! Did you see the news? Ain't that something about those old pirates still being alive after all these years? Dad? What do you think about that?"

"Sit down, Tommy, and eat," said the little boy's mother.

"Don't be so hard on the kid, Peggy," said Tommy's father.

"This boy is always off in a world of his own. He should be thinking about his books more than thinking about some old pirates, who are more than likely part of some Hollywood stunt! They're probably trying to advertise some movie or something."

"No, Mom! It's the real thing! Even the President is going to give them a big parade real soon! Tell her, Dad! Please tell her Dad !"

"Stop it! Please, Tommy, stop it! I don't want to hear any more about it," replied his father. "Now, eat your dinner, Tommy."

"Man," Tommy grumbled as he looked at his dad and started to play with his food. But he couldn't eat because he was too excited.

Later that night, as they were getting ready for bed, Steve looked at Peggy as she was brushing her hair. "Honey, I was just remembering, when I was a boy just about the age of Tommy, my grandfather used to tell me stories about his Grandfather. As I recall, his name was Captain John Flenn. I wonder if that was the same guy that everybody is talking about on the news?"

"Steve, don't be foolish. There's no way that man could be your great-great-great-great-grandfather," said Peggy, her voice full of sarcasm.

Steve shrugged his shoulders and said, "Well, tomorrow, I'm going up into the attic and look into some of GrandPop's old trunks, and see if there is something that will tell me about Captain John Flenn."

"Oh, turn off the lights, Steve, and go to sleep. We'll talk about it in the morning," she said, as she got into bed.

As the Battleship U.S.S. Missouri docks in the Virginia Harbor, news people from all over the world and every kind of media known to man were there, as well as curious people with their children. More people were on the docks than ever before. They were there hoping to get a live look at the old pirates as well as to see their ship. Standing in the crowd were people from the schools and churches, city officials, Governors, and even world Leaders from other countries. It looked as if the whole world had turned out to see them.

Looking down from the deck of the Missouri was Captain John Flenn and his men. Even Captain Nash and his Lt. Gaither were looking with astonishment at the huge crowd. They were amazed at so much excitement! Tugboats were blowing their horns, fireboats were shooting water up into the air, bands were playing, flashes were going off from cameras, and TV lights were shining. One would have thought it was the 4th of July, there were so many fireworks.

"My! My!" said Captain Nash, "You certainly have caused a lot of excitement, Captain John Flenn." Standing there with their mouths open and their eyes about to pop out of their heads, John Flenn, Samooya, and the entire crew had never seen – or even dreamed about– anything like this in their entire life. The old pirates were lost for words. All they could do was look at each other and point their fingers at one thing and then another.

Without a doubt, things were happening too fast!

"Come on Dad! You promised! Come on Dad!" Tommy was pleading with his father.

"Alright Tommy, but we'd better make it quick before your mother gets back from her sister's house," Steve said.

"Gee, Dad, I'm so excited!" Tommy said, as he and his father were opening a big old trunk that was in the attic, covered with dust. "Hurry up Dad! Come on, hurry!" urged Tommy. Steve had to break the lock, since there were no keys to be found after all these years.

As the lock snapped, Steve said, "Now, I think that should do it." Then he slowly opened the trunk.

As soon as the top of the trunk went up, Tommy dived right in. He and his father began going through all kinds of old family heirlooms. Then, there it was — a picture of the famous Pirate Captain John Flenn, Samooya, and standing between the two of them was Jessica. It was their wedding picture.

"There they are, Tommy! Just as I thought. He was our ancestor, and this picture proves it!"

"Gee, Dad, it's the same men we saw on the news today at the White House with the President!"

It was hard to tell which of the two was the most affected. Steve slowly sat down on the floor with his mouth open. It took him a piece of time before he could answer his son."Yes, Tommy, you're right."

Tommy, becoming alarmed, began shaking his father as he called to him, "Dad! Dad! Are you all right?"

In a small office on Capitol Hill, some Senators were having a discussion about the upcoming elections.

"Senator Greenwood, believe me, if we don't do something about all the publicity the President is getting from the fallout of those Old Pirates, we're doomed in the coming elections."

"What do you think we should do, Bob?" asked another man in the office.

"I don't know... But, we'll have to do something. Believe me, time is running out. Just think, we had this election in the bag until the President's men got their hands on them."

"Yes, I know what you mean," said Senator Greenwood. "Even my own son is looking at the news when he's on TV with those pirates, and he is only ten years old!"

"Ladies and Gentlemen, The President of the United States of America!" came a voice from out of the loudspeaker. Walking down the aisle was the President with his First Lady and his entire Cabinet. Everyone in the banquet room at the White House began to applaud. Then the President and all his guests took their seats.

Seated at a long table was the President, Captain John Flenn, Samooya, Captain Nash, and his own 'First Mate', Lt. Gaither. Flash bulbs and TV cameras were everywhere.

By this time, the pirate crew had gotten used to all the excitement. But they were as wild as a football team trying to dance in a ballet; the men were eating with their hands, laughing and talking loudly, standing on top of the tables, and some were even throwing food at each other. All in all, everyone was having a great time. Even the President was laughing and slapping his knee. The people in TV land had never seen anything like this before. The telephones at the news stations were jumping off their hooks. It was a grand show! The world loved it!

"Look Dad! That's the same two guys we saw in the picture," said Tommy as he sat with his father and mother in front of the TV. In fact, most of the world was watching the banquet at the White House on their television sets.

"What pictures?" asked Peggy.

"Well... I took the kid up into the attic and went rummaging through some old things of Grand Pop's. I found a picture of an ancestor of mine, that my Grand Pop had told me about when I was a young boy about Tommy's age. Fortunately, I kept those old things."

"Yeah Mom! " Tommy said, jumping up and down, "Ain't that something?"

"Oh, Steve," cried Peggy. She seemed distraught as she spoke to her husband. "Do you realize what this means?"

"Yes, I do. I'll have to go to Washington, D.C. and let them know that this Great Captain John Flenn is my great-great-great-great-grandfather!"

"Can I go with you, Dad? Huh, can I?" pleaded Tommy.

"Look at you Steve, you've got this boy all steamed up. He already has too many things going through his head as it is." Peggy was obviously irritated as she continued. "Why should he be thinking about some old pirates that are probably fake — some kind of movie stunt?"

"Oh, Mom," said Tommy, "It's true! It's true! We've got the pictures to prove it! See Mom? Take a look at this!"

Looking at the picture of the three people, Peggy says, "I just can't believe it! There must be some kind of mistake. It just has to be! It just has to be!" Then she sat back down onto the couch, her mouth open, looking first at the picture, then looking back at the TV.

Meanwhile, back in that small office on Capitol Hill, Senator Greenwood was pulling out his hair with worry, as he said, "We've got to do something, men, and I mean right now!

Look at those heathens! The world's in love with them." As the group of men watched the Presidential Banquet Room on their TV, the senator was beginning to mumble rather helplessly. "He's got the entire country in the palm of his hand. We've got to do something! If not, goodbye White House!" As they directed their attention back to all the activity being shown on the television screen, there was a moment of unwelcome silence.

Then, one of the senators jumped up from the table and said, "I've got it!" Then, since he had everyone's attention, he continued, "We'll get the people from the Smithsonian Institute to give those guys and their ship a good looking over. Because I know there is no way they could be the real thing. And, if we can prove that they are not what the world thinks they are, we can discredit the President and all of his staff! Not only will we win the election; the people will run them out of town!"

Now, having a big smile on his face, Senator Greenwood said, "That's a great idea. I love it! Get on it right away! I want some results by tomorrow! Now, get to work!"

"Ladies and Gentlemen, here is a special bulletin that just came in," said the TV news announcer. "Senator Greenwood and his campaign organization have demanded a full investigation of the so-called 'pirates' who mysteriously turned up off the coast of Bermuda, and have caused so much excitement all over the world. Specialists from the Smithsonian Institute have been called in to examine these men as well as their ship. As we speak, they have been put under the custody of the Institute until the scientific results can be concluded... Now back to our regular programming."

"Dad! Did you see the news?" asked Tommy, running into the living room. Still clad in his pajamas, he jumped on the couch beside his father. He had been upstairs in his bedroom watching his own TV.

"We've got to do something about it, Tommy," said Steve as he looked at a picture of Captain John Flenn that was now sitting on top of the family's TV.

Peggy, who was upset by all the disturbance that had recently come into her usually uneventful life, spoke to her husband, "Steve, why get involved in all this mess about those pirates? Don't we have enough on our hands trying to raise our son? Why put all these thoughts about such nonsense into his head?"

"Peggy, sweetheart..." started Steve, as he tried to reason with her. "Right or wrong, John Flenn is our ancestor, and what if by some unexplained phenomena he's alive and doesn't know he has relatives in these times? That's one reason I am going to help him."

"That's it, Dad!" said Tommy, "and I am too! I'm with you, Dad!"

Looking at the two of them, Peggy knew she had to give in. But deep down inside her heart, she also wanted to help Captain John Flenn and his men. Steve thought he saw a tear in her eye when Peggy finally spoke.

"You guys are my family, and families are supposed to stick together. So, count me in too." They all gave each other a group hug, and Tommy, looking into his mother's eyes, put his arms around her neck, and with the biggest smile ever, he said, "Mom, you're the greatest!"

"Lieutenant Gaither, you are the only man for the job, " said Captain Nash.

"But why me, Captain?"

"Come on, Lieutenant — remember, you're the one who picked them up on the high sea, and you've been with them ever since. But the main reason is, they trust you," reasoned Captain Nash.

"But Captain," argued Lt. Gaither, "it broke my heart to see them under lock and key at that Smithsonian Institute, being examined like a rat or something. They must hate me for that, Sir."

"At any rate, Mr. Gaither, someone should be there to look out for their interests," said the Captain.

"Well, since you put it that way, Sir, when do I report?" he asked.

Captain Nash answered, "How about tomorrow?"

Chapter V

In the laboratory of the Smithsonian Institute, Professor Von Highlandhoff and his team of scientists were trying to examine the men, but not with much cooperation.

"Gentlemen! Please, Gentlemen! We must control ourselves!" He had to duck as one of the laughing, wild pirates threw something at his head. They were breaking up things, grabbing the female scientists, kissing and pawing over them. It might have been work for Professor Von Highlandhoff and his men, but not to the pirates. They were having the time of their lives.

In a chamber where they were holding a Senate investigation on the authenticity of Captain John Flenn and his men, Senator Greenwood had the floor. "My fellow Senators: you know as well as I that the man sitting over there could not be Captain John Flenn — The John Flenn we read about in our history books. Don't let those people fool you with their lies." Then, passing and looking over at the table at John Flenn, Samooya, and Mr. Gaither (acting as their defense counselor),

Senator Greenwood continued, "Maybe this is some Hollywood trick. Not only are they trying to fool the President, they are also trying to fool the American people as well. That's where we draw the line! I could not just sit by and let all those wonderful voters have a sham pulled on them. It is my sworn duty to protect the good old American voters of this great and grand country. He stopped, cleared his throat, and said (completely altering his tone of voice) "I mean Good Old American People."

Mr. Gaither turned to Captain Flenn and said, "Man, he's laying it on thick today."

Samooya leaned over to Mr. Gaither and said, "I don't like this man; I'm gonna go over there and break him in two!"

Grabbing Samooya by the arm in time to stop him from getting I up out of his chair, John Flenn said, "No Samooya! Let the man talk."

"But John," said Samooya, "he's telling some awful bad lies about us!"

"Yes, I know," replied John, "but I have complete faith in Mr. Gaither; he'll do right by us, just you wait and see." Looking in John's face and seeing the look in his eyes, Samooya realised his friend John Flenn knew what he was doing by putting so much trust in Mr. Gaither. So, for the time being, Samooya calmed down, and the rest of the Senate Investigation Room calmed down too.

After three days of debating, Mr. Gaither got on the floor, saying, "Gentlemen, as you know, my men and I were the ones who found these men at sea. They were picked up in the

Bermuda Triangle by our satellite orbiting in outer space, on May 5th, 1998. We all know that in that area, there have been hundreds of unanswered things happening over the years. Now, I have here a statement from a professor who is an expert in this field. I would like to read it into the record, if I may..."

Mr. Gaither started to read.

"To Whom It May Concern: In the area commonly known as The Bermuda Triangle, on the fifth day of May, in the year of our Lord, 1998, it so happened that there was an unusual turbulence in the waters at the bottom of the sea. This bottom disturbance caused a great deal of peculiar debris to surface. We found this uncommon debris floating off the coast of the Bermuda Islands.

After an extensive study by my staff and me, I am able to report to you that something strange happened, and in the near future something unusual will occur again. It's even possible for three more occurrences. This is not conclusive, but very likely."

Mr. Gaither continued, "This is signed by Dr Ralph Edwards of the O. S. State Department of Unexplained Phenomena."

Now Gentlemen, if that's not enough proof, here is another report from Professor Von Highlandhoff, Head of the Department of Research at the Smithsonian Institute. It reads:

"Dear Sirs: After many scientific experiments on clothing, weapons and parts of their ship; and DNA tests upon their persons, we find that all the above, without a doubt, are well over two, or maybe three hundred years old give or take a few years! Under the oath of perjury, I submit this statement."

After hearing these reports, everyone who was on the Investigating Committee started to look around at each other. They were unable to speak while they were digesting these outrageous statements.

Senator Greenwood jumped up, waving his hands, and shouted: "Gentlemen! Don't let this man make a fool out of you! We all know nothing can live underwater for two or three hundred years! What are you? Some kind of fools?!"

By this time, the room was in an uproar. The Chairman was beating his gavel over and over on his bench, shouting, " Order, Order! Gentlemen! We must have order."

Soon, things calmed down, and that's when Mr. Gaither said, "Gentlemen, before I rest my case, I have only one more thing I have to present to you." Then he turned and pointed to the two huge doors at the entrance of these grand chambers. At that time, the doors opened, and walking through them and down the isle were Tommy, Steven, and Peggy.

Once again, Senator Greenwood started waving his arms around and shouting, "Who are these people? What are they doing here? Who let them in? This is a closed hearing! !"

Mr. Gaither interrupted, "Gentlemen of the Senate, I would like to introduce to you the only living relatives of Captain John Flenn!"

That statement made Senator Greenwood ask, "How in God's name is it that Mr. Gaither can bring people in from off the street" – pointing his finger – "to say that this man is the long-dead Captain John Flenn?! Come on! Let's be serious! Gentlemen! Don't let him make a fool of you!"

"As I was saying, before I was interrupted... These people are the descendants of this man sitting here, Captain John Flenn! And here is the proof." He pulled out a small oil painting. "Yes, Senators, it's a picture of Captain John Flenn, Mr. Samooya, and Captain Flenn's wife, Mrs. Jessica Flenn, on their wedding day. As you can see, the defendants have on the same clothing — clothing which has been rigorously tested, as has this picture been tested, by top scientists. And the results prove that it was painted during the 1700s." Passing the portrait to them, he said, "Gentlemen, look for yourselves! "

As they passed the picture around the committee, each person could see that it was the same people. Indeed, there was now no doubt; it was true. Captain John Flenn, believe it or not, had come back from the deep blue sea, from 1743, to walk the streets of the world, in 1997!

Chapter VI

Three months had gone by since the authenticity of the pirates had been proven. Most of the excitement had died down, but the press was still having a field day talking about the pirates in the news. Talk show hosts were still inviting them onto their shows. Heads of State were giving them keys to the city. Schools were having them speak about their lives on the high seas as pirates.

Some of the men were living in plush hotels. Samooya had made such an impression with his huge size, the RWA wrestling association had given him a TV contract. He was the new Heavyweight Wrestling Champion. The world was going Samooya crazy. However, the fans, like everyone else, were very much fooled by his youthful appearance and strength, for Samooya was at least 20 years older than they thought.

Captain John Flenn was now living the life of a family man. He had moved in with his newly found relatives. But night and day he was still thinking about his dear sweet wife, Jessica, whom he had left back on the island many years ago. All she knew was that he had sailed out to sea to fight the dastardly Captain Red Dog. She had no idea that he had been dragged under the ocean in the mysterious Bermuda Triangle.

"Grand Pa," (as Tommy called his illustrious ancestor), "Please, one more time. Tell me how you sailed on the high seas back in your days. Come on, Grand Pa! Come on..."

For the one hundredth (if not more) time, John began to tell Tommy about his adventures. Each night before bed, he would tell Tommy stories about the days of old on the High Seas. It did John a world of good to tell young Tommy things about himself. Sometimes, he would add a little onto it, but for the most part, it was all true.

Tommy had a love for John Flenn that in his eyes made the old Sea Captain nothing short of a hero. After falling asleep in John's arms, the Captain would pick the young boy up, take him upstairs, and put him into bed. This became a routine for them each and every night.

Steve, seeing the strong bond between Tommy and John Flenn, felt good about his decision to bring him home to live out the rest of his days with them. And besides, he too loved hearing about John's adventures.

With Peggy, it was a different story. At first, she thought his moving in with them was a good idea. But, as time passed, she began to feel that John was a bad influence on both Tommy and Steve. Laying in bed one night, Peggy was talking to Steve, and said, "Hun, I know John is your relative, but things are getting out of hand."

Answering her with a surprised look on his face, Steve questioned her, "I don't understand, Peggy. What do you mean, things are getting out of hand? I thought you liked John as much as Tommy and-"

Peggy explained, "Liking him is not the problem, Steve. Not only do I like him, but I love him as much as both of you! It's just that he's a bad influence on Tommy."

Steve questioned her again, "What do you mean he's bad for Tommy? He loves Tommy. I don't understand!"

Peggy tried again, "All I'm saying is that he is filling his head with all those stories about his life long ago, and I can't see any value in it. All the boy thinks about is some day going back with John to a time that will never be again."

"Well, what's wrong with that, Peggy? Tommy is only a kid. He has plenty of time to grow up and make something of himself. Why not leave him alone, Peggy? Let the boy enjoy himself while he can. Remember, he's only a kid once, and only for a short time at that!"

Showing signs of exasperation, Peggy said, "He is my son too, Steve ! I say, tell John to stop telling stories to Tommy, night after night! Because, if he doesn't, he will just have to..." (she hesitates, but continues) "Well, He'll just have to leave!"

Steve was flabbergasted. "Oh Peggy! You can't be serious. I didn't think you were feeling that strongly about the whole thing."

Peggy said, with tears running down her face, "And, as for yourself, you're just as bad as Tommy! Since that old man came, you... you don't even have time for me anymore. I wish we had never brought him home." She began to cry.

Steve just lay there, looking sad, trying to figure out what to do about this unexpected situation that seemed to be breaking up his family.

In the guest room, Captain John Flenn was lying on the bed looking at the portrait of Jessica on their wedding day, standing between him and Samooya under a blossoming plum tree. His mind began to roam back to that day. It was shortly after he and his crew had settled on their island.

Things were going well for them back then. In time, all the scum of the sea knew about Captain John Flenn and his Island. It had become one of the safest places to hide. Outlaw pirates from all over the world had come to hide on John Flenn's Island. In no time at all, it became a growing community. A person could buy or sell anything there. Only the best of everything was available. And, all of it was under the control of Captain John.

Even though John was controlling everything, Jessica was controlling him! She was the ideal woman for him — strong (she could fight almost as good as any man), a dutiful wife (she kept his home exceptionally neat and clean), a great cook (Oh, what miracles she could perform with the food she set on the table), a marvelous lover (Oh, what miracles she could perform with John 's body!), and an extremely competent business woman and bookkeeper (she never lost track of any money or booty). And, to top it off, she was the most beautiful woman on the entire island, or perhaps the entire world.

Running through the door of John's huge bedroom – it took up most of the upstairs part of their inn – Jessica said, "John Flenn, I'm going to say this just one time, and no more!" John, knowing her so well, could tell by the look on her face that she was not playing. And, not only that, but she also had a small pistol in her hand!

John threw his hands into the air and said, giving her a half smile, "What? Hold on, what's wrong with you, Jessica?! Whatever you're talking about, yes! I will! I did! Or I'm going to! How do you like that?" Then he lay back against the headboard of his super-sized bed, laughing.

Looking into her eyes, he could tell she was dead serious. "You better say the right thing," Jessica said, "This time you've gone too far, John Flenn!"

"Gone too far?" I don't understand, my sweet," John stammered. "Well, what?" asked John.

Looking into his eyes, she took a deep breath and said, "John Flenn, I'm pregnant! Pregnant!"

"What?!" exclaimed John, jumping up with a big smile and a look of surprise on his face. The thought of him being a father made him grab his head and fall to the floor! As he was looking up at the ceiling, he shouted with joy, "WOW! I'M GONNA BE A FATHER!"

Then he looked over at Jessica and began to reach for her to put his arms around her. But to his surprise, she moved back and pulled back the hammer of the pistol and said, "Don't you touch me, John Flenn! I mean it! Don't touch me!"

John was becoming more confused by the minute. He looked at her with pleading eyes and said, "You wouldn't shoot your own baby's father, would you, now?"

Aiming the pistol at him, Jessica said, "I'm going to ask you a question, and you had better answer it right!"

John, knowing all the time that she would never shoot him, said, "Ask away! As I said before, whatever you want, the answer is Yes!"

Jessica, sounding peeved again, looked him sternly in the eye and retorted, "Don't give me that crap, John Flenn! Will you marry me?!"

With his arms open and falling on his knees, John said, "Jessica, you are all in God's world I'm living for YES! YES! YES!"

Jessica instantly dropped the gun and ran over to him and threw her arms around his neck. With that, they both fell to the floor, passionately kissing. Then, needless to say, they made fantastic love until the next morning.

The sound of the crowd on the TV made John come back from the flashback he was having about his beloved Jessica. Clearing his head, he began to notice that there was a familiar person on the screen. Taking a closer look, he could see that it was indeed his shipmate Samooya, in a wrestling ring with two other guys. He was holding both of them in a double headlock, one on each side of him. Crashing them both to the mat, he then jumped down on top of them both and pinned them for the count of three. The crowd went wild! People were holding up signs saying "We love you, Samooya!" Fans were trying to look and dress like him. Samooya was an RWA star!

John, with the help of Tommy, was still getting used to the idea of what TV was all about. Although, it was extremely difficult to understand or comprehend that his First Mate was a bigtime TV wrestling Star, with all the things that entailed. John may have had only a little understanding about TV, but as for some of his crew – still under the careful eye of Lt. Gaither – they didn't even try to understand anymore. They just thought it was real life in a box.

Chapter VII

Back in a plush hotel in the upper-class area of the city, the pirates were having the time of their lives. The elevators were being ridden up and down again and again. People were being harassed, especially the ladies. The pirates were pulling on them and trying to kiss them. You name it, and they were doing it. People were moving out of the hotel as fast as they were moving in. Room service was continuously running in and out of their rooms.

One pirate who had drunk too much Miller Lite and started to watch TV. While he was remote hopping, he found himself looking at an old 1930s movie, "Captain B-Zood," staring Earl Flynn. He yelled out to the other men in the room, "Look, look! Some of our mates are at sea, but somehow they are in this damnable little box from hell!" Everyone crowded around the TV, looking at it, and trying to figure out how to get the men, the ship, and the ocean out of the little box. The men walked around and around the TV set, looking upside down at it, blew their breath on it, spit on it, and some of them went so far as to hit and kick it. Nothing worked. Then all of a sudden, the scene changed and there it was. A fight!

Earl Flynn, with a bloody sword in his hand, was fighting with about ten other men. The action became too much to bear! The buccaneers began pulling out their swords. All at once, as if someone had given an order, they all began to slash and stab the TV set. Being secured in their hotel room for so long and high on Miller Lite, the pirates needed action. Spontaneously, they drew their swords and pistols and began to play fight with each other. Not trying to hurt anyone, but firing their pistols just the same. Fighting, drinking, laughing, and throwing food, or anything else they could get their hands on (lamps, tables, pillows, etc.,)

Their main objective seemed to be just to knock each other down. Soon the fight moved from the hotel rooms to the hallways, in and out of the elevators, then down the grand staircase and into the lobby. The other hotel guests were screaming and running for their lives. The hotel staff was trying to calm everyone down.

Back upstairs, in their room, two men had drunk too much beer and had passed out. Stumbling up from off the floor, each of them grabbed a beer and gulped it down. They looked at each other, then at the 'picture box'. During the previous confusion, someone had stepped on the remote control and had changed the channel. The two drunken pirates were now looking at Indians! Indians riding on horseback in full war paint! Indians riding over a hill by the hundreds! They were riding to attack a covered wagon train. After all the beer consumed by these two, no one would have been able to tell them that those wild Indians were not about to ride out of the picture box, and ride down on them! Because they were drunk, they became overly excited at the sight of their first wild Indians. The two of them pulled their flintlock pistols at the same time, and fired at those devilish, painted, wild men coming at them. Well of course, the TV went up in smoke...

None of this would have ever happened if Lt. Gaither had been there. But on that particular day, he had taken two of the men out for a treat in his new, shiny, red convertible. As they rode down the street, the two men were holding onto one another, about to wet their pants. Moving without a horse or a ship was just too much for these two pirates, fresh from another world, to accept. Gaither, just looking at these two men, knowing it was a completely new experience for them, began smiling. As he drove down the street, he started trying to explain how an automobile operates.

Not long after that, the two pirates started to relax and enjoy the ride. After a few blocks, they began to look the town over. As they pulled up to a stoplight and waited for the light to change, some teenagers in a jeep (with their radio blasting) pulled up next to them. The teenagers turned their attention to the men in the red car and shouted, "Hey, everybody! It's those pirate guys! Look! It's the pirates!" All the cars at the stoplight began looking at them and blowing their horns. Before long, there was a big traffic jam at the signal. People were jumping out of their cars, trying to get a closer look or take pictures of them. The nervous pirates were amazed by all this excitement.

After the police had cleared the crowd, the three men continued on their journey. Seeing a drive-thru, fast-food place, Lt. Gaither pulled in and got into the ordering line. The two pirates were absolutely astonished and didn't know what to make of all the new sights and strange people, places, and things. Both of them were completely speechless.

"May I take your order, please?" came a voice from out of the loudspeaker. The two men looked around trying to find where the voice was coming from.

Knowing what was on the pirates' minds, Gaither couldn't help smiling as he spoke into the speaker. "I'd like to have three double burgers, three fries, three cola drinks, and three hot fudge sundaes with a cherry on top."

The two men looked at each other and began to whisper. "I think Mr. Gaither's gone crazy." As soon as they said those words, the voice came back from the speaker, repeating his order. That's when the two men jumped over the top of Lt. Gaither's new car, pulled their swords, and began chopping away at the speaker box, saying "Run, Mr. Gaither! Run for your life! There's a ghost in that box!" Then they broke and ran through the parking lot. Gaither began to laugh, because he knew how the pirates usually reacted to things they had never experienced before.

Thinking to himself, he said "Those guys keep me laughing. After I pick up our orders, I'll drive around and pick them up. By then, they'll be ready to go back to the hotel."

Walking around in their pirate attire, the two men were drawing much attention to themselves. People were stopping their cars, and coming out of stores and residences just to get a good look at these famous outlaws. The pirates were running, trying to get away from the crowd. People were running after them. The men jumped over a fence and ducked behind some boxes. After peeping around the boxes, they saw that everyone had run past, so the two began to walk down another street. Then, of course, another surprise!

Seeing them first, one of the pirates said to his shipmate, "Now! Look to the port side, mate! Yon she blows!" The other pirate looked, then turned to his buddy and said, "What are we waiting for?!" They slowly, and with cool composure, walked towards the two young, tall, long-haired, leggy, mini-skirted prostitutes.

Driving down the street, looking for the two misplaced pirates, was Gaither. After driving through two or three lights, a left turn, then a right, Mr. Gaither spots them. "Well, I'll by damned!" he said at the sight of the two rogues walking and talking with the two prostitutes. Driving down on them and pulling to the curb, he jumped over the top of his convertible and ran over to them. "Hop in fellows... Forgive me, ladies, but not this time." He pulled them into his car and sped away.

One of the prostitutes said to the other, "Can you beat that? Those guys wanted us to do all those things, and only wanted to give us these five, phoney-looking play coins! (The coins, of course, were Spanish doubloons worth at least $5000.)

"Girl, I told you there's some weird people out tonight," said the other girl. They walked on down the street.

Pulling up in front of the hotel where the pirates were living, Lt. Gaither saw people standing outside and an army of police cars all over the street. "What the hell is going on?" he was thinking to himself, as he and the other two jumped out of his car and ran over to the hotel. To their surprise, at the front door, they saw all of their renegade buddies being put into police wagons. "What is going on?" The Lieutenant asked one of the police officers.

"These guys just trashed this hotel, and put about fifty of our men into the hospital."

"Steady up, Sir! I'm Lieutenant Gaither, second-in-command on the U.S.S. Missouri. I'm also in charge of those men."

"Sir," said the policeman, "I don't care who you are. All these people are going to jail. And, those two men with you are going also."

"Why do these two have to go with them? They were with me," objected Gaither. Nevertheless, the police were still handcuffing the other two and putting them, along with the others, into the police wagon.

"Take it up with the Judge — I'm just following orders!" answered the angry, arrogant policeman. "My boss said to arrest every pirate we saw, and not to leave a single one of them! So you had better bring a good lawyer!"

"Hey everybody! Look at this,"' said Steve, as he was looking at the five o'clock news. Peggy came in from the kitchen; Tommy and John Flenn came in from the sun porch. Steve said, "They just had a news flash about your men, John, They said there would be more information after the station break."

"What was it all about?" asked John. "It was something about-"

But before Steve could get it out of his mouth, the news announcer said, "Last night, the Grand Hotel was trashed from top to bottom by the crew of Captain John Flenn's Pirate ship, *The Golden Lass*! All the pirates were guests of the United States Government. Over fifty policemen were injured before the pirates were placed under arrest. They are being held in the downtown police station."

John Flenn jumped up saying, "I've got to get to my men!"

Tommy said, "What are we gonna do, Grand Pa?"

"I don't know! But if I know my men, they expect me to save them."

"Let me call my lawyer," said Steve.

"No! We don't have time," said John. "First, I've got to find Mr. Gaither and go by the City Auditorium to pick up Samooya !"

"Well, let's take my car," said Steve.

"Cool! Let's go!" said Tommy, only to be stopped by his mother.

"Tommy! You'll have to stay home with me!"

"Oh, Mom! Don't make me stay! I want to go with Grand Pa!"

"Tommy! Stop it! Stop it right now!" said Peggy. By the look in her eyes, John knew that she disapproved of him and her son's relationship.

"No, Tommy, you'll have to stay, this time," said Captain Flenn.

With tears running down his face, an angry Tommy said to his mother, "Why is it, Mom, you never like for me to do things with Grand Pa John? He's always been good to me, and for some reason, you don't like him! And Mom! You are wrong! You are wrong!" Then Tommy ran up the stairs and slammed the door to his room. He was still crying as he fell across his bed and began to beat his pillows. However, in a few seconds, he became very quiet.

A few minutes later, Steve was out front, blowing his car horn.

Running out of the house and jumping into the car, John said, "We'll have to get in touch with Lt. Gaither, then pick up Samooya." They began backing the car out of the driveway. But, to their surprise, Tommy had climbed down the big tree that was next to his bedroom window and ran down the drive-way. He knocked on his father's moving car window.

His small voice said, "Open the door, Dad! Open the door!"

Seeing that it was Tommy, Steve slammed on his brakes, stopped, and opened the rear door, letting his son in. Steve looked at him and said, "Tommy, what. What are you doing? Didn't your mom tell you that you can't go with us?"

"I don't care, Dad! I'm going, Dad, and that's that! I'm going so that I can help Grand Pa John !"

He looked at Tommy through his rear-view mirror, then looked at John, and said, "What can I do? He is just like me! When his mind is made up, that's it" So the three of them drove off in the direction of the police station where John's men were being held.

Arriving at the police station, they see Gaither and his attorneys walking down the police station stairs. Jumping out of the car, Captain Flenn ran over to Mr. Gaither and asked, "Where are my men?"

Mr. Gaither replied, "I have just talked to the Captain of the Police, and he said they are going to have to ship them to a special place because they are making too much trouble in the station. Man, he is mad as hell!"

Steve asked him when they would be shipping them out, and Lt. Gaither said, "Later on tonight. In the meantime, I'm going to the Smithsonian for a meeting, where I I'm going to try to get immunity for them. But I have to tell you John, it doesn't look good."

"I've got to get my men out of there," said John, as he and Steve ran and jumped back into the car. "

"Where to now?" asked Steve.

John said, "To the City Auditorium."

Samooya was in the ring with three men penned on the ropes. The crowd was wild, yelling encouragement to Samooya. John, Steve, and Tommy, ran down to the ringside; they worked their way over to the ring. Looking down and seeing John, Samooya says "Hey Captain! What are you doing here?"

Looking at the sight of Samooya dressed up in his spandex wrestling costume, John had to laugh as he said, "Came to get you. The police are holding our men. You and I are the only ones left, so we're going to have to save them. Now, get this thing over with and come on!"

"Aye! Aye! Captain!" replied Samooya. With his extraordinary strength turned up a notch, Samooya picks up all three men at the same time and throws them out of the ring, knocking them out. The crowd almost tore the place down as he jumped over the ropes and ran down the aisle with John, Steve, and Tommy. Before the announcer could pronounce him the winner of the match, they were out of the auditorium.

Parked on a back street across from the police station, the four of them were watching the pirates being loaded into police vans. "What are we gonna do now?" asked Samooya.

"I've got a plan," said John. "When I walk over to the policemen, I want you to grab them from behind, then we'll get the drop on them. Then, after we've freed the men, we'll take the vans. And Steve, you can follow us in your car."

"Got it," said Steve.

"Aye, Aye, Captain, Sir! " responded Samooya.

"What you want me to do Grand Pa?" asked Tommy.

"You stay here with your father and keep the car running, Okay?"

"Aye, Aye, Captain Grand Pa, Sir!" answered Tommy, as he bravely saluted and tried to stand taller than he really was.

John smiled and patted Tommy on the head as he said to him, "Good Boy!"

He then walked over in the direction of the policeman loading his men into the trucks. As he came closer, one of the policemen saw him and said, "Here comes another one of them — let's get him!" When they made a break for John, Samooya surprisingly wrapped his long arms around them so tightly that the policemen passed out. When the men saw what was happening, they began to jump the other policemen.

In short order, all of the policemen were laid out on the ground, and the pirates were in their vans singing old pirate songs, as they followed John Flenn in Steve's car, driving wildly to an unknown destination.

"Where to now, John?" asked Steve.

John, knowing they were in big trouble, said, "The Smithsonian Institute"

"Why the Smithsonian Institute?" asked Steve.

"To pick up Mr. Gaither. He's there trying to persuade them to let us go. And, we have to find out where they have our ship. We've had enough of all this!"

"But, where would you go, even if you could get to your ship?" asked Steve.

"Home!"

"Home?" Steve asked incredulously. "That is impossible, John. You know as well as I do how you got here. You're from another time. You can't, get back!"

"I'm talking about the sea. We are seamen, and our home is the sea, so get me there fast!"

Driving down the freeway in the car, was John, Samooya, Steve, and Tommy, followed by his entire pirate crew in the police vans. Never having driven anything with wheels before, the pirates were swerving all over the highway. From the sky, a police helicopter spotted them. Not long after that, there were dozens of police cars chasing them, with lights flashing, and sirens crying — the whole nine yards. What a parade!

Arriving at the Smithsonian, John and Samooya ran up the steps of the building and broke open the front doors. But, never having been in this part of the museum, the pirates were amazed at the sights. Following behind John, but still looking around, the pirates were still spooked. Although they were trying to hurry, the men were astonished at the sight of airplanes, old spaceships, old cars, and so many other things, but when they got to a big display of dinosaurs, they just flipped out.

They began running over each other trying to catch up with John. "Here it is, Samooya." John said. Then he began to break the lock off a big door.

"Where are we?" asked Samooya. Steve was still holding onto little Tommy's hand as he was looking for a light switch.

"As I remember, when we were here before, I saw this room and it was full of-"

Before he could say another word, Tommy had found the light switch. To everyone's surprise – except Captain John Flenn – there it was: a room full of all kinds of weapons. Machine guns, rifles, swords, daggers — you name it, and it was there." Alright, men, grab what you can, and follow me!" ordered John Flenn. The men went crazy. They were grabbing everything and running behind Steve, Tommy, Samooya, and their Captain.

Outside the Smithsonian, an army of police were arriving and running through the front door. In the meantime, Steve had found a map of the Institute and had located another exit. They managed to get out before the police caught up with them. They piled into the car and the vans and headed for the docks. John yelled for Steve to follow him as he led them to the marine vessels.

It wasn't long before John found his beautiful *Golden Lass* anchored at the dock. "Hurry, Men! Get on board!" shouted John.

Joyfully running with their arms full of all kinds of modern weapons, John's men boarded their old pirate ship. Still standing on the dock, John shouted the order for his men to cast off. Looking at Steve, John grabbed his hand and said, "Well, this looks like this is it..."

Steve, with tears in his eyes, said "I'm going to miss you, John Flenn."

John replied, "Steve, you know I feel the same way. But we both know that this is not the place or time for men like me."

Looking into each other's eyes, these two fine men, though separated by four generations, yet so very much alike, grabbed each other in a big hug.

Knowing they were still in danger, and that time was running out, Samooya shouts, "Captain, I don't think I can hold this gate and keep them back much longer!" He had been holding back the police, who were beating at the gates of the dock area.

Not seeing Tommy, John asked Steve, "Where's Tommy? He was right here a minute ago."

Looking around, Steve said, "He's probably hiding. He's at that age, he couldn't bear to have you see him cry."

"Well, tell him Grand Pa will always be thinking about him. He's a fine young man." With that, He turned and ran for the ship, with Samooya close behind him.

The ship's crew were pulling up the anchors as their ship began moving from the dock. Running towards the ship, Samooya asks, "Are you ready?"

"I'm as ready as I'll ever be." With that, both of them at the same time leapt off the dock and sailed through the air. Both men, side-by-side grabbed hold of the anchor chain. Then, waving back at Steve, they threw a salute to each other as they were being hauled up along with the anchor.

Breaking through the gates, too late to stop the ship, the police stood at the dock looking at the little pirate ship sailing away.

Back again at sea, in full sail, the *Golden Lass* and her crew were once again free.

The pirates were ecstatic with happiness. The men were dancing and singing their great old seaman songs as they were attending to their duties. "It feels great to be back at sea again, don't it Captain?" said Samooya, as he manned the big wheel.

"Yes, Samooya, there's nothing like the open ocean," replied the Captain.

"Which direction, Captain?"

"I don't know... Just out to sea! Anywhere is better than back there!"

When a few miles out, one of the men came running across the deck. "Captain! Captain!" he exclaimed. "Look what we found below!"

Standing there between two sailors, looking down, was Tommy. With a surprised look on his face, Captain Elenn looked down at the lad and asked, "What are you doing here?"

"Err... well... I... I slipped on board with the crew when no one was looking."

"We will have to take him back Samooya, his dad is probably in a panic looking for him," said John.

"No! Don't! Please, Grand Pa! I want to be with you!" pleaded Tommy.

Looking into his sad eyes, Captain Flenn said, "You can't go with us, Tommy. We have no place to go but onto the high seas."

"That's all right, Grand Pa, I've always wanted to be a pirate like you. Don't take me back."

At that, all the men joined in. "Yeah, Captain, don't take him back. Let the boy stay. He's a good lad; we'll take good care of him."

Captain John looked at the men and looked down at Tommy, and said, "Hard rudder left Mr. Samooya! Out to the deep!"

Then the entire crew shouted with excitement, and they were off to the high seas... and freedom.

Chapter VIII

Days passed before the sight of any land, until a seaman on top of the crow's nest yelled, "Land Ahoy, Land Ahoy!"

Captain Flenn, looking through his old spyglass, said, "I thought we were on the right course, Mr. Samooya."

"Where are we, Captain?" asked Samooya.

"If my calculations are correct," answered John, "we should be in the Bermuda Island area... but things don't look the same."

"I know, Captain," stammered Samooya, not believing his eyes. "There's a lot of strange-looking ships floating out here!"

Once again, the seaman in the crow's nest shouted, "Ship Ahoy! Ship Ahoy, Captain! To the starboard, moving fast!"

Captain Flenn turned looking through his telescope, and there they were — a police speedboat, rapidly moving in on them! The Captain started shouting orders to his men. "Full sails, men! We're going to try and outrun them! Let the mainsail out all the way! Heave to, men! Give it all you've got! Hard left rudder, Mr. Samooya! We must out-sail them!" The *Golden Lass* began to pick up speed.

Unknown to him, Steve, Peggy, and Lt. Gaither were with the police on board the police boat.

"More sails, men! More sail!" shouted John. One of the men shouted back, "We're giving it all we got, Captain!"

Tommy was so excited that he was jumping up and down. As he held onto John Flenn with one arm, he had his other arm behind his back with his fingers crossed.

On the police speedboat, Peggy and Steve were nearly out of their minds with concern for their precious son, Tommy. "We got to catch up with them! We must!" cried Peggy.

"Don't worry, lady," one of the policemen said, "There's no way they can outrun us!"

"It's all your fault, Steve. How did you let Tommy get away from you?" scolded Peggy.

"The boy will be all right; we'll have him back in no time," said Lt. Gaither.

"Why don't they stop?" asked Steve.

"They probably think we're after them," replied the policeman, "They must realize they will have to pay for what they damaged."

Once again, the man in the crow's nest yelled, "There's another ship coming up on the bow, Captain."

Now things were looking bad for Captain Fienn and his ship, until he spotted a patch of fog through his telescope. "Head into that fog, Mr. Samooya! Maybe we can loose them in there."

"Aye! Aye! Captain!"

"Left full rudder."

"Left full rudder, Sir," repeated Samooya.

"Hold it steady right there, Mr. Samooya," directed Captain John. "Steady as she goes!"

By sailing into the fog bank, the speedboat's crew could not see the little *Golden Lass*. "Where do you think they are, Lieutenant?" asked the policeman.

"I can't see a thing in this fog. Maybe we can pick them up on our sonar screen."

After searching for the little ship with no success, the policeman turned to Mr. Gaither and said, "Something must be going wrong with my sonar equipment, because we're getting a lot of static and interference."

"It looks like we've lost them in the fog, Captain," said Samooya, with a big grin on his face.

"Yeah, I hope so! But if we did, then they fell for the oldest trick in the book." Then, with the tension broken, the renegades, as well as Tommy, started laughing.

As the *Golden Lass* slowly sailed through the thick fog, something began to happen. It was as if a big wind was blowing them around and around in a huge whirlpool. Once again, the ship was unexpectedly being sucked downward to the bottom of the ocean. The men were holding onto each other and to anything else they could hang on to. Around and around, faster and faster, the *Golden Lass* was spinning until it hit the bottom of the sea.

Then, just like it went down, it came back up! Once again, the little pirate ship had been caught up in the phenomenon of the Bermuda Triangle.

"WHAT HAPPENED, GRAND PA?" screamed little Tommy.

"I don't know Tommy, but if it's what I think, we had best get out of this fog! Right full rudder, John ordered. " Steady as she goes, Mr. Samooya."

"Aye! Aye! Sir! Got it!"

The beautiful *Golden Lass* slowly sailed out of the mist and into the sunlight. The men were looking at each other, saying, "I think I've been in this same place before. I feel strange, just like I did when we went under the last time."

"Yeah, if the same thing has happened as before, I hope those police are not still after us in that strange-looking con-traption," spoke another sailor.

"Land Ahoy!" yelled the man in the crow's nest.

"Look Captain!" Samooya stammered, "It looks like our old island!"

"By Gaud, yes, It is! Just as I thought," said John Flenn, "We're back home, men! We're back home!" The entire crew began to sing and dance to old seamen's tunes.

"What a happy day this is, Captain," shouted Samooya.

"Yes, my good man! It is indeed a happy day!" answered John. As the small ship sailed into the harbor, Captain Flenn took Tommy by the hand and pointed out the Island. Tommy, his eyes wide with excitement, asked, "What do you mean, Grand Pa John?"

With adoration in his eyes as he spoke with his grandson, he explained, "Well, Tommy, whatever belongs to me belongs to you too, so everything you see is mine. Therefore, everything you see belongs to you."

Tommy, not really comprehending the enormous meaning of all this, dismissed it, and got down to the real business of a child. "This ship too, Grand Pa?"

"Yes, Tommy, this ship too," laughed John.

"Wow! Well then, Grand Pa, if this ship is mine, then let me drive it!" declared Tommy.

Both John Flenn and Samooya began to laugh.

"The lad is just like you, John Flenn," everyone on the ship was saying as the young Tommy Flenn was guiding the *Golden Lass* into the Island harbor. John, standing back watching Tommy at the helm, began to have flashbacks about the time he was a boy on a ship with Sir Richard Ball. How happy he had been to be on that ship with such a great man — the same way Tommy was happy to be here with him.

Then he was thinking about his beloved Jessica. Would she still be there? Was she still alive? Maybe she had grown old or even might be dead. There is no way he could know because no one had ever experienced such a phenomenon before. But one thing John did know: he was back and on his way home, and had with him his great-great-great-great-grandson of whom he was very proud.

Chapter IX

Landing on the sandy beach and walking through the jungle to the edge of his town, Captain Flenn held up his hand for his men to stop, and said to Samooya, "Something is wrong!"

"I know, I feel the same way Captain," declared Samooya.

"What is it, Grand Pa?"

"I don't know Tommy, but something ain't right. I don't see anyone walking in the streets, and it's late in the day. People should be shopping, walking around, and doing things. It looks like a ghost town."

A group of men walked slowly through the town looking high and low for some sign of life. "Let's go over to the Bull's Head Inn, and see if anyone is there," suggested one of the crew. So the men slowly and carefully walked in the direction of the Inn.

Soon they were peeping into the windows. "Look Samooya — most of the people are locked up in chains," uttered John.

Samooya quietly answered "Yes, I see."

"Not only that! There's some men from off Captain Red Dog's Ship holding firearms on them," whispered John.

"And that can only mean that Red Dog must have taken over the island since we've been gone."

"We've got to do something about it, Captain," declared Samooya.

Captain John Flenn, almost by instinct, knew what to do. He started issuing orders: "Samooya, you take half the men and go around the back. When I fire one shot, that will be the signal to rush in and overpower them. Okay, move!" commanded the Captain. He looked at Tommy and said, "Tommy, you stay here. 1 don't want you to get hurt."

"I can fight, Grand Pa," protested Tommy. "Let me go!"
"NO! Not this time!" John spoke sternly to the young boy, "Now, you listen to me! If you're going to be a good sailor, you will have to follow orders!"

"Well, since you put it that way, I'll stay," murmured Tommy.

"Now that's a good boy." John then took his pistol, held it in the air, and fired.

"That's the signal," announced Samooya. "Come on, men, let's go!" The men inside the inn were taken by surprise when John's men rushed them. There was a quick, short fight. Red Dog's men knew they couldn't win, so they gave up quickly.

"Let those people out of those rooms and the cellar," shouted Flenn. He grabbed one of Red Dog's men and demanded, "Where is Jessica, you dog, tell me now!" The man looked as if he was not going to talk, so Flenn slapped him across the face with his hand and grilled him again.

The man answered, "Red Dog will be back today, and he's got Jessica with him. Not only that, he's got two shiploads of fighting men with him... You don't have a chance, John Flenn."

"Take him and put him with the others! Put them all in chains!" conveyed an angry Captain John Flenn.

Running into the inn and jumping up into John's arms was Tommy. "Grand Pa! I saw the whole thing — you were the greatest, Grand Pa! You were Great!"

Smiling at Tommy, John replied, "You were, too, Tommy. You did just what I ordered you to do. That means you are now a first-class seaman!"

"Oh, Thanks, Grand Pa," Tommy announced as he hugged his neck tightly.

"Now, men, we have to move fast. Samooya, you and some of the men go down to the ship and get those weapons we took from the Smithsonian. Hurry back! I've got a big surprise for Captain Red Dog and his so-called powerful gang of sea dogs. I want the rest of you men to go through the town and free all our people. Tell all those who can fight to come and give us a hand. The rest of them take into the jungle and hide them until it's safe for them to come out. Now move!" ordered Captain Flenn. "Tommy, you go into the jungle with the women and children."

"No! No! No, Grand Pa, I can fight like you," asserted Tommy.

"There is no need of talking, Tommy," replied Captain John.

"But Why, Grand Pa? I'm not a baby."

"I know, Tommy, that's why I'm sending you with them — so you can take care of them," cajoled the Captain.

"Oh, now I've got it. That's real cool, Grand Pa. Come on, men!" said Tommy, proudly walking away.

Looking at Tommy and smiling, Captain Flenn began to set traps for Red Dog and his men.

Just as the man said, Red Dog came sailing into the harbor with two shiploads of men. Looking through his telescope, Red Dog exclaimed, "There's my island. I've got all the men I need, a big navy, an island, and a sweet lady. He looked over at Jessica, who was standing next to him. She had been kidnapped by Red Dog when he found out that John Flenn had been lost at sea.

Not knowing John Flenn was back and laying a trap for Red Dog, Jessica was thinking, "If only John were alive, he would make this low-down dog of the sea pay for all the wrong he has done. It makes me feel sick to think of all the people he hanged on our beautiful island, just so he could take over. And now there's no one left to stop him."

"Wench," Grabbing Jessica by the arm and pulling her, Red Dog demands, "Come here!" Closer to him, he says, "Look! All this you see out there belongs to me now) How do you like me now? I'm the new king of the sea! Ha, ha, ha!" He tries to kiss Jessica, only to be slapped across the face.

"Take your hands off me you dog!" cried Jessica.

"Captain, what do you want me to do with these weapons?" asked one of Flenn's men, returning from their ship that was hidden in the harbor.

"Give everyone a weapon and follow me down to the shore," said Captain Flenn.

"But Captain, the men don't want to use those weapons," said another. John was getting anxious; "Why not?" he asked.

The sailor answered, "Because they don't know how!"

As soon as he said that, Tommy came running up to his grandfather, full of excitement saying, "Grand Pa! Grand Pa, I do! I know how!"

John, showing his exasperation, turned to his grand son, "Tommy! What are you doing here?"

Tommy, feeling contrite and sort of fearful of his grand father, spoke quietly; "Well, Grand Pa, I just couldn't stay back there. It made me feel like a baby. I want to fight like you! And besides, I can show you how to use all of those weapons anyway."

Samooya interrupted, "Well, I think you should let the kid help us, Captain. Anyway, we don't have much time!"

Reluctantly, John said, "Okay, Tommy, get to work! Let's see what you know!"

Tommy took a machine gun, loaded it, and pulled the trigger. Bullets went flying all over the place. People were ducking under wagons, diving behind trees, and taking cover any place they could. When the smoke cleared, Tommy said, with a smile, "How was that, Grand Pa?"

Peeping out from behind a barrel, John Flenn announced, "Wow! I'm next!"

Still smiling, Tommy took a hand grenade and pulled out the pin. He then threw it into a small pond. BOOM! went the grenade, and out of the pond came gallons of water and assorted fish. The sound of the explosion made everybody dive for cover again.

"See Grand Pa, it's nothing to it. I told you I knew how."

It wasn't very long before all of John Flenn's men knew how to use the modern firearms. Then it was time for all of them to take their positions that had been assigned to them by Captain Flenn and Samooya. They were ready!

One of John's men was in a tall tree as a lookout. They didn't have to wait long for the lookout's warning. "Ahoy! Red Dog's ship is sailing into the harbor! He will be landing on the beach very soon now!" John Flenn and his men were ready to do battle with Red Dog and his bloodthirsty crew. Most of the men had women and kids to get home to. This was one battle they were anxious to have at, and to have finished.

"Keep your head down, Tommy," ordered John. Tommy was lying by his side on the beach, in a trench they had dug in the sand.

"Don't worry about me, Grand Pa, I won't get in your way."

After looking the situation over, John was satisfied that all was in order and that Tommy was as safe as possible under the circumstances. As he looked at Tommy, he asked him, "How did a boy your age know how to use such powerful weapons?"

Tommy, proud that he had been able to help, said, "I've seen lots of John Wayne movies."

Captain John looked at Tommy and asked, "Who the hell is John Wayne?"

At last, Red Dog and his marauders were landing on the beach. Jessica's hands were tied, and she was being pulled along by Red Dog. After dragging her through the water and reaching the beach, Captain Red Dog commanded, "Some of you lads take this woman up to the Inn for me. It'll be your heads if something happens to her, or if she gets away." Two men grabbed her by her arms, and kicking and screaming, they dragged her away.

Captain Red Dog started screaming orders. "Alright, you no good sea dogs, get encamped on this beach and set up a place to stick all these supplies. The rest of you, grab your weapons and lets take over the rest of this island. Kill everybody that looks like they might cause trouble. Burn the whole town down! I want to see blood, lots of blood! Then, these fool people will know that Captain Red Dog is the king of these islands! So, come on you lazy fools, let's get the job done! Kill! Kill! Kill them all!"

The men began running and screaming in the direction of the town, waving their swords and pistols in the air. They were like wild animals. Red Dog was standing on top of a big rock waving his men on, yelling "Kill! Kill!"

Not expecting to be confronted by any resistance – especially not from all the ordinary people Captain John Flenn had waiting for them – Red Dog's men ran without caution and the first wave of renegades fell into a camouflaged ditch, covered with leaves, and full of snakes. Their screaming and crying for help was the first indication that someone was ready for their invasion, and they had walked into a trap.

Red Dog was shrieking, "Batch out, men! There's traps everywhere!" In his mind, he knew it could be only one man — Captain John Flenn. His thoughts were running crazy... "How could it be? Everyone knew John Flenn's ship and all of his crew were hundreds of fathoms under the ocean..." But somehow this type of trickery had the smell of only one person: John Flenn!

Another group of John's men were acting as decoys. Three of Red men started chasing them. They were excited to at last be chasing their enemies. They were running, waving their swords and pistols in the air, firing. They played this chasing game until they ran into another trap! A big net dropped on top of them, and pulled them up into a tall tree.

Seeing these things happen to his men, an enraged Red Dog bellowed at his First Mate, "We'll wait here! You run back to the beach and bring back the men! I want them all to come here! Someone is trying to stop me from taking over! This is MY island! GO! Be quick about it! Go! You damn fool! Hurry! Run!"

Still dragging Jessica by the rope, the two men of Red Dog's gang were just about out of the jungle, on their way to the Bull's Head Inn. One of the men, looking around, spooked and with fear in his eyes, said, "I thought I heard something over in those bushes!"

Before he could say anything else, Samooya and John dived down on top of them and knocked them out. Running over to John, with her hands still tied, was Jessica. She could not believe her eyes at the sight of him standing there with a big smile on his face. John grabs her, picks her up into the air, and they both spin around. Putting her back down, he looks into her deep blue eyes. Feeling so much joy, the two lovers began to kiss. With tears running down her face, Jessica says, "John! I thought you were dead! This can't be real! Tell me it's not all a dream. Please, oh please, John, tell me you are real!"

Untying her hands, John began to laugh. "No, my love, it is not a dream."

Then, without warning, Jessica's attitude changed from glad, to mad as a wildcat! She slapped John across the face. John fell back with a surprised look in his eyes, and incredulously asked, "What was that for?"

Jessica, standing there with her hands on her hips, but with undisguised love in her eyes, stated, "I've been crying night and day thinking you were dead! Everyone says you're at the bottom of the sea. Now, after I just about gave up hope, here you pop up! How could you do that to me?" As she looked into John's eyes again, she threw her arms around his neck with such force that they both fell to the ground. She kissed him all over his face, over and over again.

There was a snapping sound in the bushes! Samooya kneeled down on one knee and touched both of them, as he spoke quietly, "Hold it, both of you! Hold it down! I think I hear something over there." John pulled out his sword as he and Samooya slowly crept over to the bush. Reaching with one hand, behind a big bush, Samooya picks up a small body.

"Tommy!" both of them exclaimed. With his feet kicking in the air, Tommy pleaded, put me down, I'm on your side."

Dropping him to the ground, Samooya asked, "Didn't we tell you to stay back there until we came back, little captain?"

Getting up and running over to John, Tommy (his eyes begging for understanding) implored, "Grand Pa, I was thinking you and Samooya must need help, that's why I didn't stay put."

"Who is this sweet little boy, John?" asked Jessica.

John said, " Jessica, this is Tommy, and he's your-" Before he could get it out, a bullet rang past their heads. "Get Down!" shouted John.

Everyone hit the ground! Like rain, Red Dog's men were charging in on them. As fast as lightning, pulling out their swords, John and Samooya were engaged in battle. Jessica grabbed Tommy's hand and ran for cover. John and Samooya could take care of themselves. Red Dog's men outnumbered John and Samooya ten to one. But, after a wild and bloody battle, the odds became even. Seeing there was no win for them, Red Dog's two men ran off into the jungle.

Catching up with Jessica and Tommy, John gave orders for them to go to the Bull's Head Inn and tell his men to get ready for Red Dog and his renegades. With that preparation made, he and Samooya ran deeper into the jungle.

"Here they come, Captain, they're here! " the lookout for Red Dog's camp shouted! Wild and traitorous looking (after listening to Red Dog's insane howling for blood), these men were running through the jungle with no thought in mind except to kill!

In the meantime, standing there, acting as if he were Superman, Red Dog was thinking, "Whoever it is that's trying to stand in my way can't stop me now! With all these men, nothing can stop me!"

One of his men came running up to him, pointing his finger at two injured and exhausted men who were stumbling back into their camp, looking as if they had just seen a ghost, saying, "Captain! Captain! He's back! He's back!" They then collapsed to the ground.

Bending over, grabbing and shaking them, he shrieked, "Who, you fool! Who?"

One of these quivering bodies looked up at Red Dog and whimpered, " John Flenn."

Standing there, looking like the crazy man he was, Red Dog said, "I knew it. Damn that John Flenn! This time I'll kill him myself! Come on, men, break camp! Get up, you good-for-nothing sea dogs! Get a move on! Show me you've got a backbone! I want to see blood! Nothing but blood! I'll pay a king's ransom for the head of that scum of a sea rat, John Flenn! NOW MOVE IT!"

Red Dog's hired men were running in all directions, with muskets, pistols, swords, spears, and homemade bombs — all kinds of weapons of their time. Little did this bloodthirsty army know that they were in for the surprise of their life!

"Is everybody in place?" asked Captain Flenn.

"Yes, Captain, and Tommy and Jessica are safe in a room upstairs in the Bull's Head Inn," said Samooya.

"Well, all we have to do now, is just wait," maintained John. His men were on top of buildings, behind wagons, behind barrels, in trees, stationed in the best of hiding places. A voice came from high up in the trees. "Get ready! Here they come, and they're coming from everywhere!"

As soon as the first wave of men ran into the town, two men unexpectedly stepped from behind a stack of boxes with machine guns. It was Captain John Flenn and his first mate, Mr. Samooya! Fire was spitting out of their barrels as if they were dragons. Men were falling all around them. Bullets were zinging and booming up against the walls and through the windows. Dust and sparks were flying all around Red Dog's men.

Even though the first wave counted to more than fifty men, fear had taken the place of bravery. One man yelled, "Run for your lives, men! It's John Flenn's ghost, and he's back from hell! Run for your life!" They scattered and began to run back into the jungle without even paying attention to their wounded. It was a slaughter.

"Get ready, everybody, they'll be back!" exclaimed John Flenn. Now, the people of the town, seeing this, began to get their courage up. They began to grab everything in sight to fight with. Seeing that more and more of the town's people were joining them, John said to Samooya "Now it looks like we might have a small chance of winning."

"Here they come!" somebody yelled. From out of the jungle, into each side of the street, Red Dog's men were swarming into town. There must have been over a hundred and fifty men in this wave, all of them shouting and shooting.

But, surprise, surprise! Less than ten of John's men sprang up out of a covered foxhole, throwing hand grenades and firing machine guns. Red Dog's men were falling all over the place. They simply could not understand what was going on. The sight of the loud and smoking machine guns was too much for them. How could so few men cause so much damage? How could so few men possibly overpower them?

Many of them – the ones that could – ran back into the jungle. But some of them were diehards. They fought their way into the town. And, with much effort, they began to pick off some of Captain Flenn's men. It took hours, but they finally took over some buildings. And now, for the first time since they landed on the beach, Red Dog had a chance to get into the battle.

Chapter X

Running back into the jungle to make a report to Red Dog was one of his men who had just left the battle in town. "Captain, we've got some men staked out in the town. Now we can take the town with one more big rush."

Looking at the man with a look of disbelief, Red Dog bellowed, "What do you mean? One more big rush? I gave you enough men to take the queen's palace. What happened to all those men, you fool?"

"But Captain," the man tried to placate his insane boss, "Those men got some strange weapons. Two of them can hold off fifty of us."

Then Red Dog, squinting his eyes and clenching his teeth, looked at the man and said, "You coward!" With that, he pulled one of his pistols and shot the man in the head. "All right, you scum of the earth, everybody get your weapons and follow me!"

He turned to one of his men and ordered him to run down to the beach and signal their ships. "I want you to tell both of them to use their cannons. Aim for the center of the town, and don't stop firing until I say so! Now! Go, you fool! Go!" Then, with the rest of his terrorized men, he stormed off to take the town and kill everyone, including Captain John Flenn.

Some of Red Dog's men were fighting from house-to-house. Blood was everywhere.

"Keep your head down, Tommy," said Jessica. She was trying to protect the boy.

"Where is Grand Pa? I've got to help him!" Tommy insisted.

"No! Come back here, Tommy!" Jessica I demanded as the boy ran across the room and jumped out of the window onto the roof. Crawling on top of the roof, Tommy saw a wagon full of hay. He jumped into it, and from there, he jumped onto the ground and ran across the street.

Knowing the boy was in danger, Jessica climbed through the window and did the same thing that Tommy did.

Running under wagons and between running horses, Tommy, while ducking bullets, looked for Captain Flenn. One of Red Dog's men saw the boy from a doorway. Tommy saw the man running in his direction with a dagger in his hand. Tommy ran into an old, burned-out storefront and hid in a corner. The old, cruel-thinking pirate slowly walks through the dimly lit store saying, "Come here, little boy, I won't hurt you. Come on out, you little brat! Come out!"

Suddenly, he sees Tommy! Slowly, he lifts up his dagger and begins to creep closer and closer until he can almost grab him!

Standing there trembling, Tommy began to think fast. "I've got it!" He reached into his pocket and pulled out his Batman, penlight. It was his good-luck piece he always kept with him. Moving fast, he flicked it on, then he shone the powerful light beam into the surprised pirate's face. Because he had never seen any kind of flashlight before, the pirate dropped his dagger, turned around, and ran.

Not understanding what happened, Tommy ran behind the old pirate, holding the light beam on him. The pirate was so afraid that he was falling over things, trying to get away from the little boy who had turned into a demon! The old pirate was pinned up against the wall, trembling. Tommy was walking toward him with the light in his face, trying to make it to the door so he could get out. But, before he could get to the door, his trusty Batman penlight went out!

The old pirate knew this was his chance; he turned around and began to run toward Tommy. Tommy, shaking his penlight, knew something was wrong with it. He turned and ran away from the old man. Knowing the pirate was madder than ever, Tommy gave the flashlight a few more slaps across his hand, while switching it on and off. Unexpectedly, it worked again. Shining it once more in the face of the old pirate, Tommy chased the man again until he was able to get out the door to try and run away.

But the old pirate, running like a wild man behind Tommy, saw that he was near enough to grab Tommy from behind. Picking him up by the back of his neck, the pirate took out another dagger and began to move it closer to Tommy's throat. Suddenly, the old pirate dropped dead.

Tommy, lying on the ground, looked at the dead pirate and saw his mouth and eyes open, with a hole in his forehead. Running over to Tommy and picking him up, was Jessica with a smoking pistol still in her hand. "Are you all right, baby?" asked Jessica.

Throwing his arms around her neck and crying, Tommy whimpered, "Let's find my Grand Pa." They got up and ran out of the street and into the Bull's Head Inn.

Running from out of the jungle to the edge of town was Captain Red Dog himself! Sword in his hand, he was leading an army of bloodthirsty hooligans.

"Look at all those men!" exclaimed Samooya.

"Yes!" John agreed, "And there's that cold-blooded fanatic, Red Dog, in the lead."

There were so many waves of men coming from out of the jungle that they began to overrun part of the town. Men were dying all over the place. One of John's men crawled over to him and said, "They are pushing us back, Captain. What should we do?"

"Go to Plan Two," John said matter-of-factly. He then pulled out a flare gun from his waistband and shot it into the sky. That was the signal for his men, hiding in the trees with machine guns, to swing down behind Red Dog's men to out-maneuver and pin them down.

Plan Two worked just fine, of course, and they took the enemy by surprise. Red Dog's eyes were popping out of his head at the sight of men swinging through the air on vines, their guns spewing fire. (And needless to say, he had never heard guns make noises that were so loud and so horrible.) Red Dog was surrounded by the dead bodies of his men. Never had he seen so many men die in such a short period of time. The men continued to fall around him like flies.

BOOM! BOOM! went the cannons from the ships off-shore. Red Dog's man had given the signal to his ships, and they were firing on the little island town as ordered. Little did they know that all of Captain Flenn's people were on the edge of town or in the jungle; Red Dog and his men were the only one's left in the town. Cannon balls were exploding. It was horrendous! Men were flying through the air, and no matter where you looked, you saw men — men without arms, without legs, without heads. Red Dog began running for his life!

Sailing through the Bermuda Islands, hopeful that he might find some signs of the two pirate ships of Red Dog, Captain Richard Ball was, as usual, walking the deck of his ship. Looking through his telescope, he sees the flare from the secret island that John Flenn had shot into the air as a signal to attack. "Look Mr. Peters, doesn't that look like a shooting star?"

"Indeed, it does, Captain, but it's too bright. It looks more like fireworks," replied his First. Mate.

Moments later, the sound of cannons could be heard.

"Captain, did you hear those cannons, Sir?"

"Yes, Mr. Peters," declared Captain Ball. "It sounds like it's coming from the port side. Swing the ship around sixty-five degrees, Mr. Peters, and let's take a look!"

"Fire you dog! Fire!" demanded the First Mate of Red Dog's second ship. They were following orders to fire on the town, not knowing their evil Captain was trapped there. "Don't stop firing men, cause if you do, Red Dog will cut off our heads! Fire! Fire, men! Keep Firing! Fire!"

"What's wrong with those fools? Don't they know they're blowing us off this damn island?" screamed Red Dog.

"Captain, let's git out of here while ge got a chance," said one of his men.

"No, you fool! Keep fighting! I am not going to lose my kingdom!" One could tell by the look on Red Dog's face that he had gone completely and utterly mad. Like a wild, crazy man, he was running around, cutting away at anything or anyone near him. His frightened men were running away from him out of the town and into the jungle.

"There they are, Captain," said Mr. Peters to Captain Ball. "Yes, right you are, Mr. Peters, I see them! Run up the colors and man the guns! Now I know I've got them right where I want them!" asserted Captain Ball.

Not long after spotting the two pirate ships, the Ship of the Queen's Navy was within firing distance. "Fire men! Fire !" ordered Captain Ball. The first blast hit one of the pirate ships broadside. Water was flooding the ship, and men were jumping overboard. "Second round, men — Fire! Fire and don't stop! Keep firing until they're both at the bottom of the sea!" ordered Captain Ball.

Salvo after salvo was fired until the first ship was completely ablaze and sinking; the Royal Navy Ship turned and began to fire on the second ship. Round after round hit the pirate ship.

Soon, the Royal Navy and the renegade ships were side by side. "Prepare to board her, men," alerted Captain Ball. Firing at close range and hitting the pirate ship with each volley, the time was right for a man-to-man attack. "Are the men prepared to board her, Mr. Peters?" inquired the Navy Captain.

"Aye, aye! Sir," answered Mr. Peters.

"Then it's entirely up to you now, Mr. Peters. You know what to do."

Saluting his Captain, Mr. Peters grabbed a rope, and along with his men shouted, "Long Live the Queen!" With weapon in hand, he told the crew, "Follow me, men!" With that, Mr. Peters and his Royal Navy fighting men swung over to the pirate ship and one of the most treacherous hand-to-hand battles in naval history was taking place. Soon, there were mountains of corpses, pieces of dead bodies, and the water was filled with the floating dead.

"Look Samooya, it's Red Dog himself, and he has gone completely mad!" announced John Flenn. There he was, the most feared man on the high seas, walking around all alone, swinging his sword at the wind and giving orders to no one. "Follow me, you scum of the earth! Follow me, I'm the King of the Island! Fight Men! Fight! I want more blood! Kill them all!"

Even though no one was there but him, Red Dog was still swinging his sword, spit drooling from his mouth as he screamed obscenities at a crew that was not there. His blood-shot eyes were filled with fire. Then, as if he had seen a ghost, with his mouth open, he wiped his eyes, trying to focus because he didn't believe what he saw. There he was with a sword in his hand — Captain John Flenn, his old nemesis! John Flenn was really standing there, surrounded by dead bodies, fire, and smoke. With a look of determination on his face, he said, "So, we meet again, Red Dog!"

"Well! Well! If it ain't the great Captain John Flenn! I thought you were a hundred fathoms under the sea. Dead and gone!" said Red Dog.

"You are right! I was a hundred fathoms under the sea, but not dead! And as you can see, I'm a long way from being gone!"

Seeing what was happening, people began to come out from their hiding places into the street to see the fight of all time. Tommy and Jessica came running out of the fire-destroyed Bull's Head Inn. Tommy, seeing John, made a break for him, only to be stopped by Jessica. "It's Grand Pa! It's Grand Pa!" he cried. "No, Tommy, stay here. Grand Pa's got something he must do," explained Jessica.

"Good work, Mr. Peters! You and your men will receive a commendation for this. Not only that, but if I have anything to do with it, you will also get a promotion! Now, let's go ashore and round up what's left of Red Dog's crew," said Captain Richard Ball of the Queen's Navy.

"Aye! Aye! Sir!" And so Captain Ball and Mr. Peters took some of the crew ashore to round up the stragglers of the outlaw pirates from Red Dog's army. With that accomplished, they began to make their way through the jungle to take over the secret town that belonged to Captain John Flenn.

Chapter XI

Back in town, John Flenn and Red Dog, after looking each other over, started walking toward one another. Red Dog pulled his pistol, only to have it shot out of his hand by John. "I could have put that ball between your eyes, Red Dog!" announced John. "But that would be too easy for you. I'm going to cut you up piece by piece."

Holding his wounded hand after dropping one of his pistols, he was still carrying several weapons on his person as he did at all times. Red Dog gave him a disdainful smile and said, "How dare you think you can cross swords with me, you fool!" He ran towards John, swinging his sword and screaming, making a wild right side slash, only to miss. John made a thrust at Red Dog, then a slash to the left, and a slash to the right. It looked as if he was taking control, only to be kicked in the stomach by Red Dog.

Falling to the ground, John threw sand into Red Dog's face and kicked him away. Getting up from the ground and rushing towards each other, they crossed blades up and down the street. Running and jumping up onto a stack of boxes, trying to get the upper hand, Red Dog pulled another of his pistols and fired at John, only to hit a big bell that was in the middle of town.

This bell was used to warn the townspeople in case of an emergency, such as a hurricane or tidal wave. It was also used to warn the people in case of an invasion. The sound of the ball from Red Dog's flintlock pistol was so loud that it was heard over the entire island. On the beach, rounding up the rest of the smugglers and putting them in chains, Mr. Peters turned to Captain Ball and asked, "Did you hear that, sound? Captain?"

"Yes, Mr. Peters"

"What do you think it was?"

Mr. Peters suggested, "Maybe a bell? It sounded like a bell"

"Yeah, I think so," agreed Captain Ball. "I know somewhere on this island, there's supposed to be a secret town that belonged to John Flenn. That bell proves there must be, as some kind of a warning signal."

Mr. Peters asked, "Where do you think it came from?"

A pensive Captain Ball, pointing, says, "I think it came from over in that direction. Let's leave a small detail of men here to finish shipping these prisoners out, and we'll take the rest of our men to search for that town."

Mr. Peters concedes, "Good idea. Since Red Dog isn't here, he must be hiding out in that town."

Captain Ball orders, "Hurry up, men, we'd better get a move on! "

With Red Dog's blood dripping from his saber, John was completely destroying him with every blow. Trying to end it, John thrust at him, only to break his blade. Seeing this, Red Dog began to crawl backwards, trying to get away from him. The two men fought for so long that one would think it was never going to end. Up the street, then back down the street, also in and out of buildings, as well as on top of buildings, they eventually fought their way out of town and down to the beach.

Red Dog kicked John in the face as he climbed on top of some rocks. Grabbing hold of his foot, John pulled Red Dog back down. Now, they were both fighting for their lives on instinct alone. Both men were out of breath and completely exhausted. Then John grabbed Red Dog by the throat and threw him onto the ground. The two men rolled over and over. John was on top, but Red Dog turned him over again. This time, Red Dog was on top. But John, with a good right hand, hit Red Dog in the mouth, knocking out his front teeth. This almost knocked him out, but he only fell against a big rock.

Capturing small groups of Red Dog's men as they made their way through the jungle, Captain Ball had at last found John Flenn's secret town. After surrounding it, they moved in. He sees some of John Flenn's men and some of the townspeople standing at the bottom of a cliff at the edge of the ocean. They are looking up at the two men who are still fighting.

Jessica, seeing Captain Ball, knew it was the end of their days as outlaws. Taking Tommy by the hand, she walked over to him and said, '*You must be Captain Richard Ball. Looking down at her and the little boy, he took off his hat, and with respect, he addressed her, "You must be Mrs. Jessica Flenn."

A bit surprised, Jessica asks, "How did you know that?"

"I've known John Flenn for years, and he has always had class," asserted Captain Ball. "You know, it's a shame he drowned at sea. I wanted to take him in and give him a fair trial. Now it's too late. But I'm still looking for that scurvy cutthroat, Red Dog! There is a reward of 50,000 pounds and amnesty for anyone who brings him in, dead or alive. 1 hope I get my hands on him, to rid the world and the high seas of his evil!"

"Well today might be your lucky day, Captain," Jessica said, as she went on to inform him, "Do you see those two men up there fighting? Well, one of them is Red Dog, and the other man is my husband, John Flenn."

Captain Ball and Mr. Peters stood there looking up at the two fighting men, with a look of disbelief.

Mr. Peters finally broke the silence and asked, "Sir, do you want me to take some men and climb up there and arrest them both? "

A pensive Captain Ball answered, "No, Mr. Peters, let my cabin boy of many years ago," referring to Flenn, "take care of that no-good, bloodthirsty, scum of the sea!"

With blood running from his mouth and nose, Red Dog slams John to the ground; he kicks him in the face, then dives to the ground and picks up the dagger that he had dropped during the struggle. Getting to his feet, John Flenn, though stumbling and weak, checks Red Dog's arm and bends it backward. John then flips him over his head, and Red Dog crashes to the ground onto his back. Red Dog sees a large stone lying on the ground, a few inches from where he had landed. He crawls to the stone, picks it up, and struggles to his feet.

At the same time, John, though still on his feet, was struggling to catch his breath. He tumbles backward against a huge rock, and sees Red Dog standing at the edge of the cliff with the big stone raised over his head, about to throw it at him. So John, with his last stumbling effort, and moving as fast as a cat, dives into Red Dog. The momentum of his diving and tackling motion took both of them over the cliff!

Down they went into the sea, still holding onto each other as they went under the water.

The men were still fighting each other while under the surface. Both men were choking each other. Then, with a free hand, Red Dog pulls another small dagger from his boot and tries to stab John! But, grabbing his arm, John broke Red Dog's wrist, attempting to take the dagger away from him. With one last desperate effort, John stabbed Red Dog in the heart. As John began to swim to the surface, he could see Red Dog with his eyes still open, descending limp and lifeless to the bottom.

After seeing both men fall off the cliff and into the ocean below, they waited several minutes. But neither of the men came to the surface. Both Tommy and Jessica began to weep. She wrapped her arms around Tommy, and in an effort to console herself and the boy, she said, "Lord, how we'll miss him. But, just having the privilege of knowing him has been a blessing — what a fine man he was." They both stood there crying and holding onto each other.

Captain Ball was thinking, "If only we could find his body, I could take it back to England and give him a proper funeral, with all the honors for the job he has done in helping to clean up this region. He was the only one able to clean up scum like Red Dog and his men. They were a traitorous, thieving, blood-letting, raping, and ravaging group. The world is certainly better off without the likes of them." His thoughts continued ... "I was grieving previously for the loss of John Flenn, but now that I have seen him alive, and yet, I have now actually witnessed his death. Somehow, it seems a bigger loss this time."

They were all standing on the beach, looking sadly out to sea, when out of the water, walking toward them, was the one and only Captain John Flenn! Seeing him, yet not believing his eyes, Tommy said "Grand Pa?" He and Jessica simultaneously ran across the sand and into the water. All of them – Tommy, Jessica, and John – fell into each other's arms, and into the water. They were all kissing each other and crying. What a reunion!

Chapter XII

In a cabin on the Royal Navy Ship of Captain Richard Ball, on the way to England, we find Tommy, Jessica and John Flenn.

"Grand Pa, you're a hero," said Tommy.

"How about that? But you're a hero too," said John.

"I am, Grand Pa?" asked Tommy.

Jessica and John were looking down at him with love and concern in their eyes, and John said, "If it wasn't for you, we wouldn't have been able to take on Red Dog and all those men."

Jessica interrupted, "All right, the both of you, tell me how did you guys get together? And John my love, to where did you and your ship disappear for such a long time?"

Looking at each other, John said, "Is a long, long story, so you better have a seat."

After taking a seat, Jessica looked at both of them and said, "Come on, you guys, I want to hear all of it."

"Well, you asked for it," said John. Then he started off by saying, "As you know, we were sailing off the coast of..."

Three days later, John was still telling Jessica all about the new, modern world he and his men had unexpectedly experienced. "Now you see why everyone thought we were dead, and also why Tommy calls me Grand Pa."

"That's right," said Tommy, with a big smile.

Sitting there with her mouth open, looking first at John, then at Tommy, Jessica had stars in her big, bright eyes. "So that makes me Tommy's great-great-great-great-grandmother! WOW!" She sat silent for a minute or two, then, looking at her beloved John, she said, "If anyone else in this whole world had told me this story, I never would have believed them. But I know you would never in a million years be untruthful to me. How incredibly fortunate and grateful I am that you returned to me and brought me this beautiful child of the future. God, how I love you, John Flenn!"

Back in London, England, we find John, Jessica, and Tommy, behind the huge double doors of the Royal Hall of Justice. They were dressed as if they were royalty. John, as he paced back and forth, was thinking, "I wonder what's taking them so long to make up their minds?"

Jessica, looking in a mirror, was thinking, "I hope this dress looks good enough, and my hair ... sometimes I can't do a thing with my hair."

Tommy was thinking, wondering where his good-luck Batman penlight was. He hadn't seen it since they left the island.

Each of them was in their own little world, and no one was talking.

A Royal Guard came through the door and said "We're ready for you now, Captain Flenn. Follow me." He opened the huge double doors and began to lead the three of them down a long aisle with a red carpet rolled all the way down to the end of the great hall. As the three of them slowly walked past the Royal Assembly of the Queen, who were standing on both sides of the red carpet, a voice made an announcement, "Here Ye! Here Ye! The Honorable Captain John Flenn and Company!"

After the long walk down the aisle with the trumpets blowing, the three of them were standing in front of the Queen of England! Standing beside the Queen as she was sitting on her Royal Throne, was Sir Richard Ball, Captain of the Queen's Navy.

The three of them bowed to the Queen, and she acknowledged them in return. Then she spoke.

"You may approach, John Flenn."

Taking three steps, he kneeled and kissed the Queen's ring. She said, "I understand you, along with Sir Richard Ball, helped get rid of that rogue, Red Dog, and his marauders, thereby cleaning up the high seas, are you not?"

John humbly responded, "It is as you say, Your Majesty."

"I also understand that you were an outlaw with a price on your head," said the Queen.

"That is also true, Your Majesty," he quietly replied.

The Queen, looking in his eyes, and then looking at Sir Richard, said, "Several years ago, I made a proclamation that states: 'Anyone who captures Red Dog and his men would receive 50,000 pounds and amnesty for their service'." Then she looked at Sir Guy Hunt and, with a smile, said, "Proclamation granted!"

She asks John for his sword, which he hands to her. The Queen then orders him to kneel, and touching the tip of the sword on both shoulders and the top of his head, she announces: "Rise, Sir John Flenn. You are now a Knight in the service of your beloved England! And, with all honor, I am granting you the commission of Captain in the Queen's Navy."

Sir John Flenn kissed the Queen's Royal Ring and took three steps backward and stood at attention. Sir Richard Ball looked over at Sir Guy Hunt and winked with a smile.

Looking at both Jessica and Tommy, the Queen, with a smile, asks Sir Richard, "Who are these people?"

Sir Richard stepped in front of the Queen and said, "Your Majesty, these people are also responsible for cleaning up the pirates in that area."

The Queen said, "You may approach, young lady."

Jessica took three steps and gracefully bowed to the Queen.

"You are such a beautiful young lady, and as I understand, also very brave. Now, for someone who has given so much to her country, I think it would be proper for your country to give you something back. So, I'm granting you the title of Duchess of..." She stopped and turned to Sir Richard Ball and whispered, "Where did you say she was from?"

Sir Richard whispered back, "She is from a small county called Humberpoole, your majesty."

The Queen continued, "Oh yes, I'm granting you the title of Duchess of Humberpoole, and all your properties will be returned to you."

Jessica bowed and took three steps backward.

At long last she looked at Tommy with a very big smile, saying, "Young man, would you do me the honor of stepping up to my throne?"

Looking down, with his knees knocking, he takes three steps, then very slowly bows. "Well, young man, I understand that you are the real hero."

"I don't know, Miss Queen," said Tommy. This made everyone in the great hall, even the Queen, roar with laughter.

After regaining her composure, she said, "For all that I have heard about you, and how brave you are, young man, what can I do for you? Just name it, and it is yours."

Tommy looked at the Queen and asked, "Anything?"

"Yes, young man, anything!" declared the Queen.

"Well ... I ... well ... uh ... Miss Queen," said Tommy nervously, "if it's all right with you, I would like to have a portrait of all of us together, and for us to ride with you in your Royal Coach, please."

The surprised Queen responded, "You are such a sweet lad. Why not? Sir Guy! Order for you to take care of all the arrangements."

A few weeks later, people were lined up and down the streets waiting to have a look at the Royal Coach, led by the

Royal Equestrian Guard, with their country's heroes riding alongside their Queen. There was much excitement in the air. Someone shouted, "Here they come!" Everyone who was standing at the Gates of the Royal Palace began to cheer and wave their hands. The drummers and the trumpeters played and marched through the gates and down into the streets of London. They were followed by a troop of Royal Guards on horseback. Then the crowd began screaming, cheering, and applauding. Some people were even crying at the sight of the Royal Coach with their heroes inside.

Tommy was all smiles as he sat beside the Queen. Looking across the coach at Jessica, who was sitting between Sir Captain John Flenn and the new Admiral of the Queen's Navy, Sir Richard Ball, he shouted, "Wow, Miss Queen, you are the greatest!" Then he gave her a big hug!

Finally, after parading through all of London, the Royal Coach stopped at the Royal Harbor, and everyone stepped out. Pointing her finger at a new, fully-rigged warship – the size of which made his other ship with one main sail look like a mere toy – this new warship was rigged with four main sails. The Queen said to Sir John Flenn, "Captain Flenn, how can you be a sea captain without a ship? So, what do you think of this one?"

John Flenn's eyes were beaming at the wonderful sight of the surprise. Then the Queen dismissed him and said, "Captain Sir John Flenn, go with God's speed."

On board his new ship with his formerly-pirate crew, John, with his arms around both Jessica and Tommy, looked out at the sea. While staring at the reflection of the moon on the water, he says to his First Mate, "Mr. Samooya, how do you like our new ship?"

Standing behind the big wheel, Samooya said, "I love it, Captain. It floats as smooth as a bird. Where to now? Captain?"

John looked up at the stars and said, "Out to sea, Mr. Samooya, Out to Sea! Then set course for the Bermuda Islands! We must find that fog bank! I believe it was God's instrument for time travel. We must trust the fog to take us, once again, to that new world we found before. As sure as the Good Lord brought Tommy back here with us, he will make sure he is returned to his own home and family. After all, Tommy is the future. He was only loaned to us for a brief second in the space of God's time."

Gene "Poo Poo Man" Anderson is a longtime figure in the world of funk music, best known for his work with George Clinton's legendary Parliament-Funkadelic collective and the P-Funk All-Stars. A vocalist, performer, and storyteller with a signature larger-than-life presence, Anderson contributed to the evolution of the P-Funk sound during its most influential years, sharing stages and studios with icons such as George Clinton, Bootsy Collins, and other members of the funk movement.

His first book, "Raper's Delight: The Birth of Hip Hop", details his experience as one of the fuirst record promoters of that genre. His memoir "Sonny and Me + Redd" reflects his personal experiences with heavyweight boxing champion Sonny Liston and comedian Redd Foxx, offering rare firsthand insight into two towering figures of American entertainment. His work blends humor, grit, and lived experience, capturing the spirit of the eras and personalities he encountered.

A lifelong creative force, Anderson continues to write, perform, and preserve the stories of the artists and communities that shaped him. That creativity overflows into fiction as well, and more on that can be found in the Foreword of this book.

His books are available from **Amorphous Publishing Guild** as well as book retailers and online sellers around the world. For more information, visit

TheGeneAndersonStory.Com

THE TRILOGY
The Adventures of
Captain
Star
& The Amazing Dr. ZUNTOR
THE TWO DUDERYON WARRIORS
Written By
Gene Poo Poo Man Anderson

THE BIRTH OF HIP HOP
" RAPPER'S DELIGHT "
The
GENE ANDERSON
Story

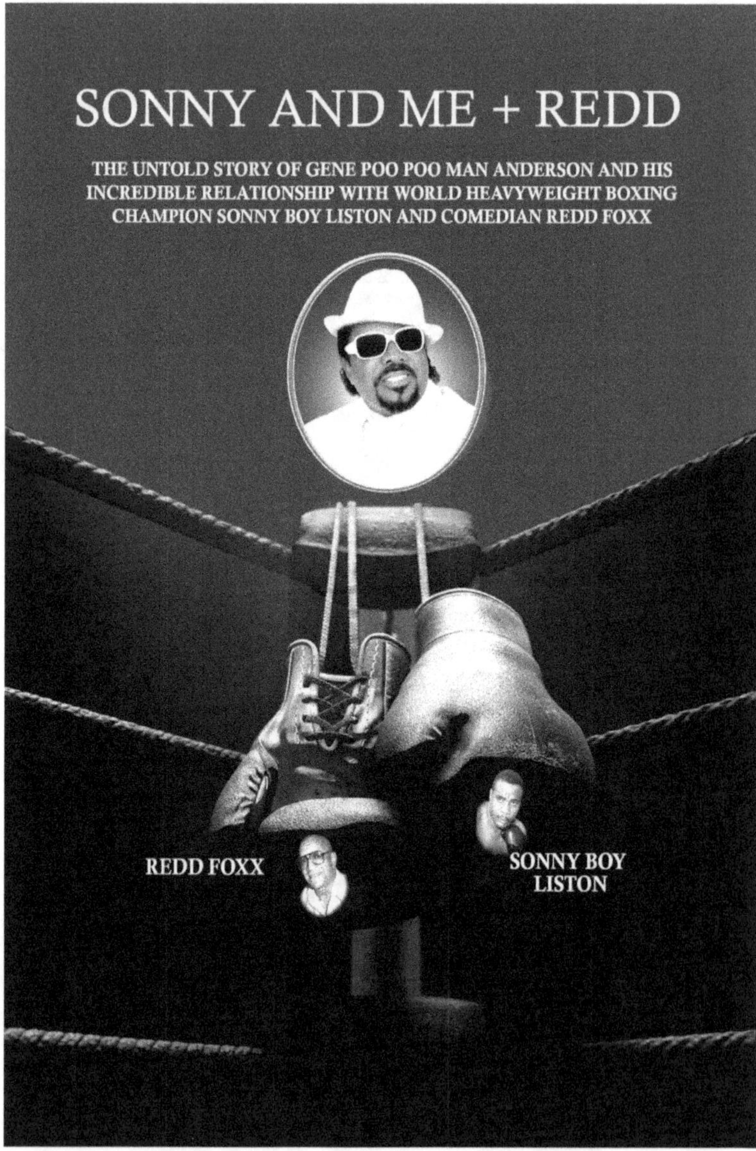
SONNY AND ME + REDD
THE UNTOLD STORY OF GENE POO POO MAN ANDERSON AND HIS
INCREDIBLE RELATIONSHIP WITH WORLD HEAVYWEIGHT BOXING
CHAMPION SONNY BOY LISTON AND COMEDIAN REDD FOXX
REDD FOXX
SONNY BOY
LISTON